# EVERYONE'S BARKING MAD FOR
# KNITBᵒNE PEPPER GHOST DOG

USBORNE

# KNITBONE PEPPER

# GHOST DOG

## The Silver Phantom

By Claire Barker   Illustrated by Ross Collins

# Contents

## Chapter 1

# DOG 'N' BONE

Knitbone Pepper sat in the hallway and stared hard at the telephone. All his instincts told him that important news was on its way to Starcross. He could feel a Big Bark tickling inside him like a sneeze, bursting to get out. He checked his symptoms one more time and did a little sum, just to be sure:

Tingling tail + fizzing whiskers + itching nose + twitching ears = 5, 4, 3, 2, 1...

*Riiing–riiing!* The telephone went off like an alarm clock, rattling the hall table. *Riiing–riiing!*

"WOOFWOOFWOOFWOOF!"

Knitbone Pepper liked barking. He liked chasing sticks and being stroked in just the right way; he liked wagging his tail and jumping up at the letter box. In fact Knitbone Pepper was just like any normal dog except for one thing: he was dead. All his friends were dead too, except for his favourite, who was both human and very much alive.

"WINNIE, IT'S THE PHONE! IT'S THE PHONE, WINNIE!" barked Knitbone, bouncing joyfully around the table.

Winnie Pepper appeared at the top

of the wide staircase. "It's alright, Knitbone! Good boy – I'm coming!" She hopped onto the banister and whizzed down to the bottom, her plaits flying. At this moment a gaggle of feathery, furry ghosts appeared at the top of the stairs. Known as Beloveds – the spirits of Pepper pets from down the centuries – they waddled, flapped, hopped and bumped down the steps, determined not to miss out on the action.

"Wait for us!" called Martin the hamster. "It might be Roojo or Bertie! What if they are planning on bringing Circus Tombellini back to Starcross for the spring? Roll up, roll up!" he said, somersaulting down the stairs. "There's nothing more thrilling than having a friendly ghost tiger to stay!"

Gabriel the goose honked as he flapped down the stairway. "What if it's about more books for the library? A librarian can never have too many books, you know."

"You already have four thousand and seventy-four library books." Valentine the hare loped down to the bottom step and stroked his ears. "Personally I hope it's about my whisker curlers."

"Eez probably Moon, callin' to say she miss Orlando." In a single bound the little monkey leaped onto the chandelier, causing the crystal to clatter and tinkle. "One day she might come back, clippy-cloppy hoofs, bells all tinkly." He gave one big swing and dropped to the floor with a wistful sigh. "I loff that pretty pony."

At the bottom of the stairs there was a general crush as the ghosts clambered over each other to get close to the receiver.

"Beloveds, please be sensible," woofed Knitbone sternly. "Can't you see that Winnie is about to speak? It is probably very important Starcross business."

Winnie picked up the receiver. "Hello! Starcross Hall," she trilled, "Winifred Pepper speaking. How may I help you?"

Knitbone looked up adoringly at Winnie, wagging his tail for all he was worth. He knew that using a telephone was very complicated because there were numbers and a lot of noise. *Winnie Pepper is the cleverest girl in all the world,* he thought proudly, *and I am the luckiest dog because she is my best friend.*

"You'd like to speak to Lord Pepper? Yes, of course," continued Winnie. "Hold on, I'll just get him." Winnie put her hand over the mouthpiece and bellowed down the corridor. "DA-AD! It's for you!"

Lord Pepper popped his head around the door

of the ballroom. All morning he had been busy alphabetizing his vast collection of hats. He made a point of cataloguing them daily; sometimes by colour, age, or even by the number of stains. It gave him endless joy and he never *ever* got bored.

"Dad! There's a woman on the telephone for you!"

Lord Pepper shuffled across the hallway in his slippers, moving at a snail's pace. He didn't trust machines, even though this particular telephone had been in the hallway since 1927. He held it up to his ear like a soggy cucumber.

"Yes, this is Lord Hector Merriweather Pepper. To whom am

I speaking? Who? Hattie? I see…oh yes…" He straightened up and his face broke into a wide smile. "Oh, goodness. Well, now you put it like that then it does sound very interesting indeed… Documents? Well, not official documents but… It doesn't matter, you say? Oh, well that's alright then… Haunted? No, don't be silly…"

Valentine rolled his eyes. "Hattie? I bet I know what that will be about…"

"Not books, that's for sure." Gabriel honked in disappointment and slipped to the floor.

"Hats of course," sighed Martin, kicking his sword. "It'll be about hats. It's always about hats."

Orlando's bottom lip wobbled and he was about to say something about missing Moon again when Winnie swept him up and put him on her shoulder.

"Come on, everyone," she whispered, heading back up the stairs, "let's go and finish off our game of cards and leave Dad and Hattie to it."

## Chapter 2

# FAN-TASTIC

The game was just getting going when the attic door flew open. Winnie's parents burst in, shiny-eyed and rosy-cheeked. "THERE you are, Winnie! We have some very exciting news!" Lady Pepper's eye was drawn to the six hands of cards fanned out neatly on the floor. "Goodness, dear, are you playing cards on your own again?"

Winnie rolled her eyes at the ghosts and they giggled. She'd tried telling her parents about the house ghosts in the past but they didn't want to listen. She had patiently explained the facts several times: that there were five ghosts, that they were called Beloveds and that they were the spirits of her ancestors' pets, including her own dearly departed dog Knitbone. But Lord and Lady Pepper believed her stories to be evidence of a powerful imagination, an inherited family trait – like freckles or red hair.

"So, tell me about the exciting news," Winnie said, changing the subject. "Are you going to be on the cover of *Hats Monthly* again?"

"Sadly no, but I think you will find this *even more* exciting," said Lady Pepper, turning to her husband. "Tell her, Hector." They exchanged starry-eyed glances and Lord Pepper took a deep breath, ready to break the news.

"The lady on the telephone was calling from a *television company*," said Lord Pepper. "She said that they want to use Starcross Hall as the location for…" He paused for dramatic effect.

"For what?" asked Winnie.

"For the Spring Special of...*JUNK PALACE!*"

The Beloveds sat up and gasped. Channel Twelve's *Junk Palace*? That was their favourite TV show and they watched it every single week, while stuffing their faces with ginger biscuits. It was a programme where people brought in their battered family heirlooms, no matter how strange or broken, to be valued by experts. All the visitors hoped they were going to discover that their precious treasures were ancient artefacts and were worth millions of pounds. But they never were, which was sort of the point, hence the name.

The programme made perfect watching for ghosts because, having been around for such a long time, the Beloveds knew a lot about antiques and were certain they knew more than the experts. They liked to offer their own opinions, often at high volume. The highlight of

the show was when the experts got it wrong
and then they could all blow raspberries at the
screen and make a hullabaloo. On Sunday
evenings there was always a squabble to get the
best position in front of the TV. The very idea of
*Junk Palace* coming to Starcross was thrilling
beyond words.

"But why do they want to film it here?" asked Winnie, glancing up at the cobwebs in the corners. Lately, the Beloveds had been much more interested in adventure than housework. "Did you tell them the hat exhibition won't be open until the summer?"

"Of course! But they didn't mind about that. Hattie – the researcher – said that she'd heard all about our hoard of Vincent Van Fluff paintings. Apparently their sale was the talk of the antiques world for months. Not only that, but she knew *all* about the hat exhibition and Circus Tombellini *and* all about the Night of a Billion Stars. She'd really done her homework." Lord Pepper straightened his favourite wizard hat and puffed up with pride. "She said we have *a reputation for fun*. She said that Starcross, being over 950 years old, was a perfect location for a show about antique items. She said it was *authentic* and that's what their viewers liked."

"But the Spring Special, Dad? That's the biggest show of the year!" Winnie was a huge fan of the programme too and had seen it take place in lots of impressive locations. "We'll have to clean up," she said, looking at the biscuit wrappers littering the floor. "When it was in the grounds of Frumpington Manor they had waiters with little silver trays handing out cheese and pineapple on sticks."

"Well, now it's our turn," said Lady Pepper, folding her arms in a way that Winnie knew meant business. "We're just as good as the Frumpingtons. This house has been standing for longer and, as Hattie pointed out on the phone, it has a particularly interesting history."

"Absolutely," added Lord Pepper. "For three days we must honk the Pepper horn loud and proud! *HONK HONK!* Eh? Tip top!" Winnie's parents giggled, slammed the door behind them and dust exploded everywhere.

Winnie turned to the Beloveds, her hair sprinkled with plaster. They were bursting with excitement.

"BUT WE LOVE THAT SHOW!" honked Gabriel, flapping his wings. "I can't believe they

are coming here, to our humble stately home!"

"Humble's about right," said Winnie. "It's not as bad as it used to be. At least the bats have moved out of the kitchen."

"Don't worry, Winnie," woofed Knitbone. "We've cleaned it up before and we can do it again. Anyway, *Junk Palace* is supposed to be rough around the edges. You know the show's famous motto." They all chimed together as one. "*Wonky chair? Battered chalice? Bring your treasure to* Junk Palace!"

"Do you remember," chuckled Valentine, "that episode where they got really excited about that rare and valuable Anglo-Saxon marriage bowl?"

Orlando tittered behind his hand. "Was just old potty. Tee-hee!"

"And there was the time when they said that cuckoo clock was Elizabethan, and when it opened a Lego bird popped out?"

"We should be the experts on that show," said Valentine. "We know more about history than they do."

Martin rubbed his tummy and it let out a growl. "All this excitement is making me hungry."

"You're *always* hungry," Winnie smiled. She stood up and opened the wardrobe doors wide. It was stacked from floor to ceiling with ginger biscuits. "Ginger curl, ginger cream, ginger nut, gingerbread or ginger snap?" she asked.

"Ummm, a selection I think," said Martin. Being a hamster and a natural hoarder, he had personally filled the cupboard to bursting with a variety of delicious biscuity treats.

Knitbone wagged his tail and helped himself to a ginger nut. "Yum! No other biscuit makes a ghost feel more alive!"

"You know," said Gabriel, spluttering biscuit crumbs across the abandoned card game, "this is our chance to dig out some of our treasures and show them off. You'll help won't you, Winnie?"

At this Orlando abruptly stopped eating and sat bolt upright. He got up and disappeared from the room for a moment. Within seconds he was back, wearing a hopeful expression and dragging a clanking handbag.

Winnie smiled at the little monkey's stash of precious treasure. "Yes, Orlando, I'm sure the experts will be very interested in your spoon collection."

"You see, eez *finest* and most *beautifullest* collection of spoons," he explained, stroking the bag.

"Yes, thank you, Orlando," said Valentine, rolling his eyes.

"Eez *shiniest* of all ze spoons."

"*Thank you,* Orlando," said Gabriel.

Orlando paused and took a deep breath. Then he added, "Eez *nicest* spoons. In the whole spooniverse."

"YES, THANK YOU, ORLANDO!" everyone chorused and they collapsed into fits of giggles on the attic floor.

## Chapter 3

# TV TIMES

One week later, in a cloud of gravel dust, a convoy of television crew vans bearing the *Junk Palace* logo roared up the drive.

"There are more people than I thought there would be," said Knitbone, panting with excitement and pressing his nose to Winnie's bedroom window. "There's at least fifty of them out there." In no time at all members of the crew started setting up big white tents and the place began to buzz with activity.

"It takes a big team to make a show like this," said Gabriel knowledgeably, flicking through a book with his beak. "I've been researching it in my *Telly Magic* annual. There are all sorts of people with funny names that don't make sense, like best boy and gaffer. There's a fluffy microphone thing called a boom. There's a costume lady and a make-up person. There's a producer, a researcher, a director and, of course, camera people." He shut the annual and looked very solemn and wise. "A lot of work goes into making a television programme, you know."

"Imagine, Winnie!" said Knitbone, sitting up and turning to look at her. "When you're on the television, I'll be able to watch you in two places at once!" He began to write something on the blackboard on the back of her bedroom door.

"Me?" Winnie looked alarmed. "Oh no, Knitbone, I can't imagine I'll be on the television." Winnie looked at her reflection in the wardrobe mirror. She had a smudge of mud on her nose and her hair stuck up. "Do you really think they'll ask me?"

"They would be MAD not to ask you," said Knitbone, his face a picture of seriousness. "Look, I've done the sums." He pointed to the blackboard.

WinNiePepper + television = STAR ☆

"It's perfectly simple. You can't argue with arithmetic." And everyone agreed.

"Actually I think *I* might be suited to a career in television," said Valentine, stroking his ears. "I was always being asked to model for medieval tapestries and it's probably much the same sort of thing."

Martin was about to say something controversial when the front doorbell rang. "That must be them," woofed Knitbone. They all leaped to their feet and raced downstairs. Winnie's parents were already standing in the hallway, shaking hands vigorously with the crew.

"Welcome to Starcross Hall," said Lord Pepper. "We are the Peppers. This is my lovely wife, Lady Isadora." Lady Pepper curtsied and bowed simultaneously. "And this is my daughter, Lady Winifred Clementine Violet Araminta Pepper, heir to Starcross Hall." Winnie shuffled forward, feeling suddenly shy.

"Hello," said the man. "My name is Toby and I'm the director of *Junk Palace*. And this," he said, gesturing to a red-haired woman to his side, "is Hattie, our researcher. She's the woman-in-the-know and the person you've got to thank for introducing us to the wonder that is Starcross Hall."

"Hello, Peppers!" The woman leaned forward and put out her hand. "We spoke on the telephone.

I can't tell you how great it is to meet you. Thank you so much for agreeing to be the location for the Spring Special. It's my job to find the story behind the property and – boy – do you have some stories! It's really excting to finally be here in person." Her eyes roved over the hallway, over the chandelier and the portraits of long-dead relatives lining the walls. "I feel at home already."

Inexplicably, Knitbone felt a tiny growl winkling up from his paws. He blushed beneath his fur – this was very bad timing. Where had it come from? Unsettled, he brushed the feeling away and put it down to not having the right sort of ginger biscuits for breakfast.

"Hattie? What a super name!" cried Lady Pepper. "Now, where are my manners? I'll arrange for some snacks to be sent out straight away. I've just finished a dazzling batch of mossy marmalade, which tastes extraordinary on nettle crumpets."

Toby and Hattie exchanged anxious glances, protesting that they had already eaten, but it was too late. Lady Pepper trotted off into the Starcross kitchen, delighted with the opportunity to rustle up something that would create an impression.

Hattie smiled at Winnie and winked. "You look like a bright spark, young lady. I'll bet you've got some stories to tell."

Winnie blushed and giggled. "You could say that. This old place is full of secrets. We – all of us – really like watching *Junk Palace*. It's a top favourite here at Starcross."

"That's great to hear." Hattie smiled. "You know, I bet you've got lots of things you could bring along for our experts to have a look at. Like that collection of magnificent Vincent Van Fluff paintings you discovered in the attic! What was the headline again? That's it – *Cash For Stash – Family Home Saved!* You might have something else like that! And those exquisite Starcross spoons!" Orlando grinned from ear to ear. "Or maybe you could help us out with the filming over the next three days? We're always looking for great presenters, aren't we, Toby?" she winked.

"See," whispered Gabriel, dancing with excitement. "Knitbone, you were right – Winnie Pepper IS a natural born star. What do you say to that, eh?"

But Knitbone couldn't say anything because his fuzzy muzzle was clamped shut. He was still busy fighting his instincts, trying to stop the growl from escaping.

## Chapter 4

# HIDDEN TREASURE

By teatime the attic looked like an explosion in a jumble sale. The Beloveds had trawled through the house, gathered together all of their precious things and piled them into one big heap. Winnie had to shoulder-charge the door to get in.

"What's all this?" she exclaimed.

"You heard Hattie," honked Gabriel, stacking his books into a wobbly tower. "She said – and I quote – *I bet you've got lots of things you could bring along for the experts to have a look at.* Well," he said, waving his wing over the towering pile, "here's lots of things!'

There were hairdryers, a Victorian umbrella stand, a silk scarf, a lampshade, a suit of armour, an exercise bike and a deep-fat fryer. There were many, *many* things.

Orlando scooted to the very top. "Eet will be the most best and most beautiful *Junk Palace* ever," he said, doing a headstand on an upturned flowerpot. "Eez already legendary in Orlando's heart."

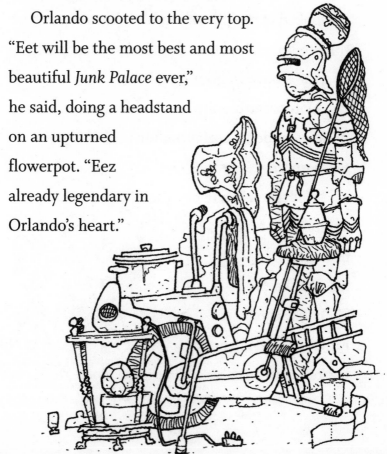

"Ah. I see," said Winnie calmly and carefully. "Well, I think if we all pick *one* item each for the programme, that would be perfect."

"Only one?" Orlando looked panicked. "But Winnie, I has twelvety-four bestest spoons!"

"Winnie's right," woofed Knitbone. "Think of all the other people bringing their things too." He looked at the pile of jumble. "They won't have time to see ALL of this. Remember, the Spring Special is only an hour long."

"Not forgetting the special feature in the middle," added Gabriel ruefully. "That always takes up time."

"Well, then," said Valentine, brushing his silky ears, "I choose this rather special silver-backed hairbrush."

"I choose this *Pepper Book of Histories*," said
Gabriel. It was a big, heavy leather-bound book.
Martin tunnelled out of the pile. "I know

what I want to show
them." He held aloft
a tiny tin soldier. It
was covered in
bashes and dents, bits
worn away by years of
play. "This was given to
me by my friend
William and it's as
precious as can be. He was the best chum…" he
sniffed and wiped his eye… "a hamster could
ever wish for." Winnie stroked Martin's furry
little head. She knew, even after all those years,
just like the others, he had never stopped
missing his special person. "I think that's a great
idea, Martin," she said, with a nod at Knitbone.
"Gifts from special friends are proper treasure."

Orlando, meanwhile, spent a long time
breathing hotly onto his spoons, polishing them
on Winnie's skirt and holding them up
to the light. Finally he
selected a tiny,
ornate teaspoon
and gave it a
little kiss.
"This one,"
he said
decisively,
"is bestest."

Winnie let out a big sigh of relief. "Finally!
Well done, everyone. I'm taking the telescope
that Knitbone dug up for me in the
conservatory." She turned to Knitbone. "What
about you? Is there anything you'd like to ask the
experts about?"

"Yes," said Orlando. "What you choose,
woof-face?"

Knitbone pondered for a moment. Not having been a ghost for very long he didn't have many treasures, unless you counted balls, sticks and the lamb-chop bone he'd been keeping for a special occasion. But there was *one* antique in the house that he wanted to know more about. "I'd like to know more about Mrs Jones's vase."

Mrs Jones was a spider who lived in the Chinese vase on the downstairs hall table. Like the Beloveds she was a ghost, but an entirely different sort, driven not by love but by resentment. The technical term in the ghost world was "a Bad Egg".

"Do you think that's a good idea?" asked Valentine. "That's really not going to improve her bad mood, is it?"

"Yes, why, Knitbone?" Winnie looked confused. "You know Mrs Jones won't like her home being touched."

"Well," said Knitbone, noticing the surprised faces around him, "I just thought that it might be helpful to know a bit more about her vase. This is a good opportunity to ask an expert."

"Are you MAD?" asked Martin, slashing his sword back and forth. "After all the trouble she's caused round here? Have you forgotten how she nearly destroyed parts of *The Good Ghost Guide*? The one-of-a-kind manual, full of phantom facts that can't be replaced? Have you forgotten how she snitched on Moon to Galloping Jasper? She's a double-crossing snitch, she's a weasel, she's a ratfink, she's a spy and a mole, she's—"

"You know," Gabriel interrupted, "Knitbone might have a point. As we all know, these days Starcross is such a happy place. The only black cloud is Mrs Jones."

"But she'll be furious," said Winnie. "She'll never allow it."

Orlando swung across the room from beam to

beam, landing on Knitbone's back. He lifted the dog's ear and whispered something into it. As he listened, Knitbone's eyes widened. "Of course! We'll just make her sleepy with a few chocolate biscuits. You know how greedy she is. Two of those and she'll be out for the count."

"Right," said Winnie, writing down the items in a notebook. "So that's a hairbrush, a Pepper history book, a tin soldier, a telescope, a spoon and a Chinese vase." She tucked the pencil behind her ear. "I'll get this list down to Hattie and the fun can begin!"

## Chapter 5

# WARDROBE

The morning of the filming dawned bright and blue. Catkins quivered like lambs' tails and daffodils turned their golden faces to the sun. Spring had officially sprung at Starcross Hall.

By the time Lord and Lady Pepper threw the gates open, a large queue had already formed. It had begun the previous evening as hundreds of people arrived in cars and vans carrying a dazzling array of curious objects, waving their application forms and paying for tickets. A woman in a beret cycled in carrying a portrait of a cat, and another person wheeled in a shopping trolley full of kettles.

"This way, please," shouted Winnie, directing the flow of traffic. "Furniture over there, paintings over here, jewellery over beyond the gazebo! A piano made from bottletops? Next to the seashell ladder, please."

Hattie appeared carrying a clipboard and patted Winnie on the back. "Good work, young lady. Carry on like this and you'll be part of the production team in no time! In fact, you'd better have one of these." She handed Winnie a walkie-talkie stamped with the *Junk Palace* logo. "All of the crew use them."

"Wow, Hattie, thanks!" Winnie grinned from ear to ear and clipped the radio onto her belt.

"Roger that!" squeaked Martin, who was sitting on her shoulder.

"Over and out!" giggled Orlando.

"See!" woofed Knitbone, walking proudly beside Winnie. "I *said* you were a star, didn't I?"

Over on the front steps a woman was having her nose powdered and her hair brushed by the make-up lady.

"LOOK! It's her!" hissed Gabriel, starry-eyed. "That's Penelope Farthing – THE Penelope Farthing! I LOVE her!"

"Her clothes are divine," enthused Valentine. "Velvet frock coats and flying goggles go so well together!"

"I love the way she uses cockney rhyming slang," said Martin knowingly. "I was born in the East End of London before I came to Starcross, you know. Reminds me of the old days."

Knitbone cocked his head to one side. "Rhyming slang? What do you mean?"

Martin grinned. "You know, 'china plates' for mates, or 'apples and pears' for stairs." He turned back to the presenter and pressed his little hands together in anticipation. "Say the catchphrase, Penny," he said adoringly. "Say-it-say-it-say-it!"

The spotlights blazed into action as a man in headphones stepped from behind the camera. He raised his arm and began to count down on his fingers, silently mouthing, "Five...four... three...two...one..." Suddenly Penelope Farthing sprang to life and leapt to her feet like a puppet.

"WELCOME to the Spring Special of *JUNK PALACE*! This year, me ol' chinas, we're coming to you from Starcross Hall, Bartonshire, home to the Pepper family for over nine hundred and fifty years. So remember..." The cameraman zoomed in and Penny smiled a ten-thousand-watt grin down the lens, ready to be beamed into front rooms around the world.

*"Wonky chair? Battered chalice? Bring your treasure to* JUNK PALACE!"

Martin jumped up and punched the air in delight.

"And CUT! That was perfect, Penny," said Toby the director. "Now we need you over in the large furniture marquee. Someone's brought in a sideboard made of toothpicks."

The make-up lady draped a fur wrap over Penny and ushered her away.

"That was amazing," breathed Winnie.

"Glad you liked it," said a voice.

Startled, Winnie spun around. "Oh, Hattie! I didn't realize you were there. Where did you come from?"

Knitbone looked up at Hattie and felt puzzled. She was smiling and her eyes were bright. Hattie was very nice, so why did she make his fur prickle? Maybe he was coming down with something.

"Sorry to make you jump," said Hattie. "We're setting up the table for the family piece – you know, with the items you wanted to know more about? We need you over on the front lawn soon, ready to meet one of our antiques experts to discuss them."

Winnie looked at her, wide-eyed. "*Me?* On the television?"

"Yes, Winnie!" laughed Hattie. "Of course! You *are* the heir to Starcross Hall, after all. Get ready and meet us there in half an hour."

Winnie looked across at the ghosts, who were struggling to contain their excitement, and said, "What do you think she means, 'get ready'?"

Gabriel stepped forward and she could see he had his "serious beak" on. "Don't worry, Winnie, WE will be your hair-and-make-up team."

"Oh. I see. Do you think that's a good idea?"

"Really, it's no bother," said Valentine, eyeing her critically. "Grooming is something of an animal speciality. Come with us."

Twenty-eight minutes later Winnie stood in her bedroom looking at her reflection in the gold-edged mirror. After a flurry of activity the Beloveds had finally settled on her "look". Valentine had raided the dressing-up box and chosen a turquoise silk ballgown. Gabriel had picked out a tiara.

Martin had offered a pair of black army boots that he'd recently been using as a snoozing spot. Orlando had dipped his tiny monkey hands into a jar of pickled beetroot and rubbed them on her cheeks to make them rosy. Nobody had even mentioned the bit of bramble that had been stuck in her hair since the previous day.

"I'm not sure about this," said Winnie, eyeing her reflection. "Are you sure I'm not overdressed?"

Valentine tied tinsel onto the ends of her plaits. "This is perfect. It is a strong look. Television is all about making an impression."

Winnie looked at her pocket watch, the one given to her by Bertie Tombellini. They had run out of time. "What do you think, Knitbone? Do I look the part?"

"I always think you look absolutely smashing, Winnie. To my eyes you'd look a hundred times better than Penny Farthing any day, even if you were wearing a cardboard box. I want you to have this for luck." He popped his special lamb-chop bone in her pocket and she gave him a pat.

"Right," said Winnie. "Come on, time to find out more about our precious things."

## Chapter 6

# LIGHTS, CAMERA, ACTION!

Winnie felt hot under the bright lights.

"Well, well," said Penny Farthing. "Here we have some very interesting objects brought in for us by the current heir to the Starcross Estate, Lady Winifred Pepper. Might I say, what a bobby dazzler you are!"

Martin confirmed that this was a good thing and Winnie blushed beneath the beetroot. "Please, just call me Winnie."

"Well, Winnie, what treasures do we have

here? Time to find out! Over to our expert."

The hairbrush, the tin soldier, the large book, the tiny teaspoon, the telescope and the Chinese vase stood on a white tablecloth, ready for inspection.

The Beloveds could hear spider snores coming out of the vase. "How many chocolate biscuits did you give her?" whispered Martin.

"Three," whispered Knitbone. "She'll be knocked out until teatime."

The expert picked up the vase and peered inside. "Goodness, there are chocolate biscuit crumbs in here!" Everyone laughed politely. "I'm afraid this is the only amusing thing about it," he continued. "What we appear to have here is a Ming Dynasty vase dating back to the fourteenth century. There are a small number of these on the market and they are very valuable and extremely collectible. They are also widely believed to be cursed. On the bottom you will see the maker's mark in Chinese characters: FLD, which stands for Fu Lin Doom. Now recognized as a genius potter, in his day his work was extremely unpopular. See this inscription around the edge here? It says *Fill me with an eternity of misery.*"

The Beloveds looked at each other and nodded. That sounded about right.

"But this one," continued the expert, tapping the vase, making a dull *donk,* "isn't even real. It's just a cheap fake." Knitbone gave a sigh of relief. It was a mercy Mrs Jones was asleep, because there would have been a big tantrum at this news.

"Now, on to this Victorian hairbrush." The expert inspected it, turning it over in his hands with a tut. "Oh dearie me. More junk. We see a lot of these on the show. Often these things can look much more valuable than they are, I'm afraid."

Valentine clutched his ears and stamped his foot. "Sir, THAT is a solid silver hairbrush left here at Starcross by Queen Victoria herself!" Valentine folded his arms and huffed. "This man is a nincompoop."

"Oh look." The expert smiled. "A little tin soldier! I'd say this dates back to 1944 and is a classic toy from the wartime period." He inspected it carefully with his magnifying glass. "See the edges? These items are often played with until they are nearly worn out. How intriguing. Something – *HBM* – is scratched into the bottom."

"William gave it to me on my birthday," whispered Martin, bursting with pride.

The expert continued his inspection.

"It's clearly well-loved but…no…worthless junk again, I'm afraid."

Outraged, Martin charged at the man with his sword. Knitbone managed to grab him just in time, leaving the hamster's stubby little legs kicking in fury.

Next, the expert picked up Gabriel's offering and carefully turned the pages. "But *this* item is absolutely fascinating." Gabriel's chest puffed up like a giant piece of popcorn. "Oh yes, here we have histories of the Pepper family, documented through the centuries. This is a true treasure, the stories of your forebears. Of course, one day your story will be in here too, won't it, Winifred?"

Lord and Lady Pepper held hands and looked on from the sidelines, as proud as could be.

"Now, what's this? This is very unusual," he said, moving on to Winnie's telescope and peering through the eyepiece. "I'm afraid it's got me stumped. Is it made out of a drainpipe? I'd

say junk-shop curio." Winnie winked at Knitbone, because they knew better – it had belonged to her ancestor, Araminta. It was no junk-shop curio – it was a priceless medieval artefact.

Suddenly the expert's magpie eye was caught by something shiny: Orlando's tiny silver spoon. "Goodness me! Can it be true?" he exclaimed, his eyes glittering greedily. "How glorious! I've always wanted to see one of these. This is a rare and extremely collectible Elizabethan custard spoon and it's the genuine article. I'd love to own one myself! Is it for sale?" He reached out to pick it up.

"Oh…" said Winnie, suddenly aware that Orlando's fists were clenched and his left eye was twitching. "Actually, I really wouldn't do that if I were…"

But it was too late.

"GOOD LORD!" gasped the expert suddenly as Orlando unleashed a corker of a Stonking Stink. The man covered his nose with a hanky and dropped the spoon with a clatter. "UGH, what is that terrible pong? It's like old kippers…and… boiled cabbage…and dirty-sock flavoured cheese!" Tears streamed down his face. "It's like some sort of…of *weapon*!"

Orlando gave a cheery grin and folded his arms in satisfaction. "Not touch spoon. Spoon is mine. Bad man. Sorry, man."

Knitbone had missed out on the spoon action because he was distracted by something else entirely, his ears twitching back and forth. He could hear a new sound, far away but getting closer and closer. It was coming from the sky. *Something* was coming.

Penny Farthing, her smile as wide as a piano keyboard, stepped into the camera shot. "Thank you so much for bringing these fascinating objects for us to see, Lady Winifred Pepper. They've shown us a real slice of Starcross history. In fact, this leads us neatly on to the next part of

the show: our *special feature*, which this season is
heaven-sent!"

With a flourish of her arm, Penny pointed up
at the blue sky. "Ladies and gentlemen," she
cried, "I'm thrilled to be able to introduce you to
our new and remarkable *Junk Palace* feature…"
A plane burst out of the clouds and the crowd
looked up. *"THE SILVER PHANTOM!"*

A shining, roaring beast, it carved
through the sky, vapour trails streaming in
its wake, the sun's rays bouncing off its gleaming
surface. It did a loop-the-loop as everyone *ooh*ed
and *aah*ed. The plane coasted around the back of
the house and landed neatly on the front lawn in
a cordoned-off area, its propellers finally coming
to a standstill to a round of rapturous applause.

Winnie and her parents looked at each other in delight. The television company had never mentioned anything about a plane. What a surprise!

Martin gasped and jumped up and down. "Oh, my stars and buttons! That's a 1939 Twin Lightning 25!" he shouted, racing towards the cordon. "And what a corker. We had a picture of one of these on the wall when William was little! I know all about them: twin radial engines, all-metal construction with fabric-covered control surfaces and tailwheel undercarriage. Brilliant! Come on, everyone!" The ghosts and the Peppers joined the crowd pressing to get a closer look at the plane.

The door popped open and a man in flying goggles climbed out. Penny, pursued by a cameraman, marched through the crowd and held a microphone in the pilot's face.

"Hello there, and welcome to Starcross Hall!"

she said. "Can you tell us who you are and a little about this magnificent machine?"

The pilot took off his flying hat and leaned into the microphone. "Yes, hello, Penny. My name is Alan and I'm from the Royal Air Force Museum in London. I'm delighted to play a part in this most special of special features for *Junk Palace*."

"So, Alan," said Penny, looking into the camera lens, "what IS so special about this particular aircraft?"

Alan cleared his throat and began. "This is *The Silver Phantom*; a Twin Lightning 25. Records tell us that this US-built plane originally saw action in the Second World War. If you care to look here and here –" he pointed at the wing – "you will see the scars of near misses."

The crowd gasped in admiration at the dents and bullet scrapes. Martin inspected them and nodded in agreement. A Second World War expert, Martin knew everything there was to know about Spitfires, the Hurricane fighter and the Wellington bomber. He collected the information in piles of scrapbooks, which he kept in Winnie's bedroom.

"After the War ended in 1945," continued the pilot, "the plane continued to work in daredevil flying shows and on movie sets. But then

*The Silver Phantom*'s story took an even more intriguing turn."

Penny held the microphone right under his nose. "Go on," she said.

"Oooh, goody," said Martin, his little eyes shining, his paws clasped together. "Tell us more. Then I can write up a special report to go in my scrapbook."

"In 1965 this plane came up for sale. There was a lot of interest in it at the auction house but, at the last moment, according to witnesses at the time, a handsome young man strode in. He bid a bag of precious jewels – rubies, diamonds and pearls – triple the value of the top bid. But his identity has always remained a mystery, as the purchase order was signed with nothing but an X. Then, within days, both man and plane disappeared off the radar."

"Disappeared?" intoned Penny, wide-eyed and moving even closer to the camera.

"Yes," continued Alan. "Records show that the plane took off from a the military base on the seventeenth of August 1965 at 17:00 hours, but it wasn't long before all radio contact was lost. That was the last that was heard of *The Silver Phantom* and the mystery pilot for fifty years. Then, three years ago, a team of trekkers stumbled across a plane wreck, half-buried in the undergrowth of a Peruvian rainforest. The aircraft was badly damaged and, were it not for the ghost of a name on its side, its secret would have been safe for ever. With this scrap of information, a museum team was sent out to recover it. On inspecting the flight recorder we could see that it crash-landed only days after the auction. But thanks to those trekkers the mystery has been solved and this wonderful piece of history that stands before you has been restored to its former glory."

Penny reached out her arm to draw the Peppers in, still looking earnestly into the camera. "Well, that is a fascinating story, Alan, but *what has it got to do with the Peppers and Starcross Hall?*"

"Well, Penny, this wreck was most unusual because, although the wings and body were badly damaged, everything inside the cockpit was unharmed – it was like a time capsule. We found all sorts of perfectly preserved artefacts inside – the pilot's flying hat, a packet of aniseed balls and piles of adventure comics. It was as if time had stood still for fifty years."

"So were there clues to who this tragic young flying ace might have been?"

Alan reached into the inside pocket of his flying jacket. "I'm glad you asked, Penny, because we now believe we finally know the true identity of Mr X." Alan pulled out a creased black-and-white photograph. "*This* was found tucked inside one of the comics." The camera zoomed in on the faded image. It revealed a small boy sitting on

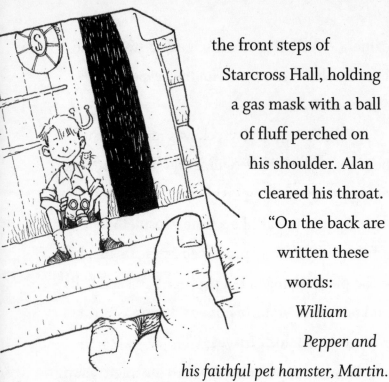

the front steps of Starcross Hall, holding a gas mask with a ball of fluff perched on his shoulder. Alan cleared his throat. "On the back are written these words:

*William Pepper and his faithful pet hamster, Martin. Starcross Hall, 1945."*

Martin gasped and keeled over in a dead faint.

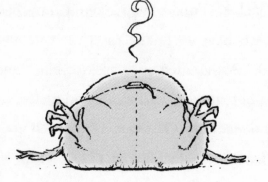

# Chapter 7

# SHELL SHOCK

Valentine and Gabriel stretchered Martin back to the house and laid him down on Winnie's bed. The filming buzzed on beneath them, forgotten in light of the shocking news.

"What a bombshell," said Gabriel, fanning Martin with his wing.

"Wake up, Martin!" woofed Knitbone.

Orlando draped himself over Martin's round tummy and began to weep and wail. "Oh no, my fatty friend is dead! OH NO NO OH NOOOO!"

"Calm down," said Knitbone. "We're ghosts –
we're dead already, remember? Martin? Snap out
of it. Can you hear me? Martin? MARTIN!"

"Perhaps we should give him an emergency
ginger biscuit," suggested Valentine. "See if that
will get him back to normal." Everyone agreed.
They tried five different sorts but nothing made
a difference.

"Do you think we should try a pink wafer?"
whispered Winnie. "Just a bit? Jolt him out of it?"

The gang looked at each other. Pink wafers were
only to be eaten in exceptional circumstances, as
they made ghosts extremely naughty. But these
were exceptional circumstances.

Orlando didn't need asking twice. He broke
a corner of pink wafer off and pushed it behind
Martin's teeth. For a while nothing happened.
Then one of Martin's eyes began to flicker.
It opened wide and began to roll around like
a marble.

"Look! He's coming back to us!" woofed Knitbone excitedly. "Martin? Can you hear us?"

"William? Are you there? Do you read me? Over and out," said Martin faintly. "William?" He blinked hard and looked up at Gabriel in confusion. "Where has William gone?"

Gabriel put his wing around the little hamster and sighed. "I'm so sorry, Martin. Don't you remember? William Pepper grew up and left Starcross years ago."

"But...but I *saw* him and he was a boy again," said Martin, his eye settling back to normal.

"No, Martin. It was just an old photograph. It's nearly seventy years old," said Valentine, as gently as he could. "It's the twenty-first century now."

"Oh," said Martin in a small, sad voice, coming to his senses. "Oh, yes. Now I remember. I don't know how I could have forgotten a thing like that. Silly me." He sat up and slipped off the bed. "I think I'd like to go back to sleep now." He rolled under the bed and lay very stiff and still.

Knitbone would never forget how sad he'd felt when he first became a ghost – how much he had missed Winnie and how the others had cheered him up. It was time to return the favour.

"Come on, Martin," he woofed. "Let's forget about the TV show for a bit. I thought we might play soldiers. You'd like that."

"Or battleships," said Gabriel encouragingly. "I'll let you win."

"No, thank you," said a little voice from under the bed. "I'd just like to be left alone."

"What about we build a tank out of matchsticks?" said Valentine, who was very good at arty things. "You can even keep it if you want."

But Orlando, a wise fool, knew that sometimes words would not do. He carefully selected a spoon out of his handbag, kissed it and slipped it gently under the bed.

"Poor Martin," whispered Winnie, crossing over to the window and watching the show go on beneath them, the plane standing in the distance surrounded by cameras. "He and William must have been very close."

"They only had two years together, but for that time they were as close as two peas in a pod," sighed Gabriel, looking over at Valentine.

"Hang on – YOU remember William?" asked Winnie, turning to look at them in surprise.

"Your grandfather? Well, yes, of course," laughed Gabriel. "I'm three hundred and seventy-four years old, you know."

"And I'm eight hundred and twenty-seven years old," said Valentine.

Orlando counted on his fingers, tongue clamped between his teeth in concentration. "Four hundreds, one and thirty...and another one."

Winnie smiled and shook her head. "Of course. You're so alive that I forget you've been dead for centuries. I suppose you must have known all of my ancestors, then?"

"Oh yes, there have been quite a crowd," said Gabriel. He waddled over to the doorframe and pointed at the various height notches scratched into it. "Centuries of Pepper children have grown up in this very bedroom," he said, "and William was no exception."

"Tell me about Martin and William," said Winnie, sitting down cross-legged and stroking Knitbone's ears. The show wouldn't miss them for a while.

"Well now," said Gabriel, ruffling his wings and lowering his voice so as not to upset Martin any further. "Let me see…when did Martin arrive at Starcross? Ah yes, it was 1943 and young William Pepper was a child of seven. Because of the War there was a great deal of bombing in London and children were evacuated to the countryside."

"Yes, with suitcases and gas masks," said Winnie. "We've done that at school."

"But I bet you don't know that, occasionally, some animals were evacuated too. A pet shop called Martin's Animal Emporium sent all of its creatures by freight train down to Bartonshire, looking for homes until the War was over. William was terribly excited because he'd never had a pet, or even a friend for that matter – rattling around Starcross on his own."

Valentine leaned forward. "But William's father, Albert, was a very serious, strict sort and said he wasn't allowed to go down to the railway station until he had finished his lessons. By the time he got there, there was only one animal left – a baby hamster."

"Martin!" woofed Knitbone, wide-eyed.

"Yes, and they were a perfect match." Gabriel waved a wing at Valentine and Orlando. "We watched from the shadows as they stuck together

78

from the moment they woke up, to the time they went to bed. Martin always rode on William's shoulder, just like in the photograph. They had such fun – William built mazes out of cardboard boxes and wood for Martin, with tunnels to wriggle through and slides to whizz down. They made scrapbooks and filled them with clippings and facts about bombs and tanks. They could make five different types of paper plane and flew them very accurately."

"One Christmas," said Valentine, "William made a special present for Martin – a little sword and belt. He even made him a tiny soldier's helmet out of an old sardine tin." Valentine smiled. "Martin was absolutely over the moon with it."

Orlando gave a big sigh. "Once upon a time, the boy was sick, all hot and burbly and broken. Was very bad. Martin lie on his pillow, watchin' and a-watchin' until he wake up."

"Yes," remembered Valentine. "Scarlet fever, we were all very worried. The doctor kept shutting Martin in his cage but he always managed to escape. Houdini the hamster, the doctor called him! The doctor said it was the medicine that saved him, but William said he'd got better because of nurse Martin."

"As the War went on," explained Gabriel, "William and Martin stuck together like glue. They shared biscuit rations and drew up plans to defend Starcross in case of invasion. William told him all about his dreams to join the RAF when he grew up and Martin couldn't have been prouder. To put it simply, they were devoted to each other."

"Was nice," sighed Orlando. "It made me very 'appy in my tummy. It had been a long, long time since we see special friends like this." Orlando stared into the distance as if remembering someone important.

Winnie looked at Knitbone and gave him a hug. Everyone was quiet for a moment, not knowing what to say. Eventually Winnie peered under the bed. "Are you alright, Martin?"

There was no answer so Knitbone woofed, "Martin, are you awake?"

There was *still* no answer so Orlando dived beneath the bed. He popped up again straight away. "Mousie eez gone!"

Together they searched in all of Martin's favourite hiding places – in the downstairs coat cupboard, under the kitchen table, in the biscuit tin, Winnie's wellington boot – but he was nowhere to be found.

"Where IS he?" honked Gabriel. "I don't like him being on his own when he's upset. You know how gloomy he can get."

"He must be outside," said Winnie, opening the front door. "But it's not going to be easy to find a small, sad hamster in amongst all those people." The gang peered around her legs at the milling crowds outside.

Orlando gave a sad sigh. "He get squished like a party sausage."

"Don't worry," said Gabriel doubtfully. "We'll just have to find him, then and he'll be right as rain in no time, I'm sure."

The Beloveds split up and looked in different places. Winnie and Knitbone looked in the furniture marquee and Valentine and Gabriel searched the artworks tent. Orlando spent an unnecessarily long time looking at his face in the silverware. They looked and looked, called Martin's name and left trails of biscuit crumbs for him to follow.

"Where can he be?" honked Gabriel when they eventually met up, the light failing. "We've been looking all afternoon and he's nowhere to be found."

"Look!" wailed Valentine, waving a paw at the television crew, who were putting away their equipment ready to start again the following morning. "Everyone's going home. We've missed the whole day."

An idea lit up Knitbone's doggy brain. "You don't suppose he would have gone back to the plane, do you? Actually inside it? It was the last place William would have been," he went on, looking up at Winnie shyly. "It's what I would have done."

"Of course!" said Winnie. "It's so obvious! Why didn't we think of that? Let's go!"

## Chapter 8

# LOST LOVE

Luckily for Winnie and the Beloveds, Alan the pilot had been collected and taken back to his museum, so they were able to clamber unchallenged up the steps into *The Silver Phantom*. Winnie opened the door and there, just as they had hoped, was Martin. He was sitting inside William's flying hat, stroking the fur with his little paws, just visible in the gloom.

"*There* you are, Martin," said Winnie gently, "we've been looking everywhere for you. We

were so worried. Come
back to the house."

"No, thank you,"
said Martin quietly.
"I'm staying here.
This is the final resting
place of my best friend
William, so this is the place
for me from now on."

"But they'll be taking the plane away
again at the end of filming – we can't keep it,
it's only here for the show," said Winnie, looking
out of the windscreen.

"Yes, come on, Martin," said Gabriel. "It's
getting dark. What about your ginger-nut
supper? You never miss your ginger-nut supper."

"I'm not hungry."

Everyone looked at each other in shock. This
was more serious than they had thought.

Martin held up an aniseed ball like it was

treasure. "Look! I found one of these – this was William's favourite sweet!" In his little arms it looked like a bowling ball. "I think it's even been sucked." He scampered over to a locker. "And look, these too!" He opened the door and a pile of adventure comics fell out. "He kept them." Martin smiled, his eyes shining. "He kept our *Beano* and *Hotspur* comics! Proof of how important our friendship was." He lifted and turned the pages like sails. "This one is all about enemy intelligence and the Pigeons of Doom and this one is about bouncing bombs. It takes me straight back to the good old days when we were boy and hamster, hamster and boy."

Valentine stepped forward with a sigh. "It doesn't do to live in the past, you know. Anyway, William was a grown-up when he left Starcross, not a boy. Things change."

"Yes, Martin," said Gabriel. He paused for a moment, thinking of his own special person.

"Those days are gone."

"Do you think I don't know that?" Martin hugged the flying hat and gave a sad, trembly sigh. "But I always hoped that, after he'd finished having very important adventures out in the world, he'd come back home to Starcross." Martin looked up, his eyes very shiny. "It wouldn't have mattered if he couldn't *see* me, I just wanted to be near him." Martin gulped down a sob. "But now I know for sure he's *never* coming back and I'll never see him *ever, ever* again!"

"Martin," said Gabriel as kindly as he could, "stop this. You know it will only make you sad. Like Valentine says, it's a bad idea to live in the past."

Martin's expression suddenly darkened as he stood up and turned to Gabriel, pointing his sword and narrowing his eyes. "Live in the past? You're a fine one to talk. That's ALL we do! If you hadn't noticed, we're *ghosts*! It's alright for you lot, you all lived for ages. Hamsters only get a few years, even fewer if they happen to choke on a particularly delicious party snack. Every single second of my life with William was precious. You'll *never* understand."

"Martin," woofed Knitbone, wagging his tail nervously and trying to make peace, "come inside and have a biscuit."

But Martin swung round and pressed the tip of his sword into Knitbone's nose. "And as for you, DOG…" His little face was screwed up with resentment. "YOU have STILL GOT your special person. So you can shut your big, hairy face."

Everyone gasped. No one ever just called Knitbone "dog".

"Steady on, Martin," said Gabriel. This wasn't like him at all.

Martin sat down in the flying hat and scrubbed his tears away. "It's not fair. You don't know how I feel. I don't want to talk to any of you." He flung himself face down into the hat. "JUST GO AWAY AND LEAVE ME ALONE!"

Not wanting to make things worse, the gang plodded back to the house and upstairs to Winnie's bedroom.

"I've never seen him so upset," said Gabriel, shaking his head. "This has really hit him hard."

"That mousie-fatty-bottom," said Orlando, giving Knitbone a pat, "has spicy-spicy temper."

"I hardly know anything about William, even though he was my grandfather," said Winnie, sitting on the edge of her bed. "All I know is that he disappeared when Dad was a tiny baby." Then an idea occurred to her. "Gabriel, where's that book that we showed to the expert? Does William have an entry in the *Pepper Book of Histories*?"

Gabriel dragged the big book across the floor and turned the pages with his wingtip. He cleared his throat and read the entry out loud:

# WILLIAM MERRIWEATHER
## MAXIMILLIAN PEPPER

1936 – Born at Starcross Hall, only child of Lord
Albert and Lady Purity Pepper

1939–1945 – Second World War. William stays at
home at Starcross

1945 – War over. William sent away to boarding
school at the age of nine

1956 – Joins the Royal Air Force aged twenty

1960 – Wins the AFC medal for bravery

1964 – Marries and divorces Eidelweiss
Hoffenfeffer, Austrian duchess

1965 – Son Hector is born in Austria and sent to
live with family at Starcross. William declared
missing the same year

Interests: flying, dangerous sports and parties.

"Well," said Winnie. "That's quite a life. Goodness."

A newspaper clipping slipped out from between the pages and Gabriel inspected it. It was brown and curling at the edges and dated November 1965.

# BARTONSHIRE TIMES

## ARISTOCRATIC ADVENTURER GOES MISSING.

William Pepper, only son and heir to the Starcross Estate of Bartonshire has been officially declared missing. Lord William, who claimed to have climbed Everest barefoot and paddled down the Zambezi in a bathtub, was a notorious flying ace, explorer and adventurer. No more is known at present. The heir to the Starcross estate leaves behind a baby son named Hector. If anyone has any information please contact Finias the butler, Starcross Hall, for a reward.

"Baby Hector? That's my dad!" exclaimed Winnie.

"William sounds like a big personality," said Knitbone.

"You could say that. He was a firecracker alright," said Valentine, pulling out a box of photographs. He began to filter through them. "Look, here are some more of him... Here he is with a catapult at boarding school, and here's another in his Royal Air Force uniform, all grown up."

"He looks very smart," said Winnie, inspecting his moustache. "But he's definitely got a mischievous twinkle in his eye. He sounds like quite a handful."

"Wherever there was trouble, you'd find William right in the thick of it. And his father never approved of his behaviour," sighed Gabriel, eyeing Valentine. "They had some terrible arguments and in the end William hardly ever came home. Then one day he stormed out, never to be seen again."

Winnie took out her pocket watch and flipped it open. It was nearly bedtime and Martin *still* wasn't back.

"Knitbone," said Winnie, "it's getting really late now. Can you go and bring Martin home, please? And this time, whatever happens, don't take no for an answer, there's a good boy."

Chapter 9

# BLAST FROM THE PAST

K nitbone couldn't resist a command. He trotted down the stairs, nosed open the front door and crossed the courtyard under the starry sky.

Moonbeams bounced off the metal of *The Silver Phantom*. It looked rather eerie in the still of the night. Knitbone climbed up the ladder and peered through the hatch. He could see Martin lying on his tummy reading one of the comics by torchlight, kicking his little legs back and forth.

Knitbone crept in. "Hello, Martin. Are you ready to come home yet?"

"Oh. It's you again," said Martin flatly, flicking through the comic. "No, I'm not. I'm in the middle of a very exciting story and don't want to go to bed. William and I always stayed up past our bedtimes. We were a lot of fun like that."

Knitbone looked around, uncertain what to say next. The torch cast strange shadows around the cockpit and he felt a tingle go through him. His nose wrinkled – it smelled odd in there; of old maps and metal of course, but there was something else. One smell dominated all others, the strongest of all – aniseed. It hung thick in the air like fog. Normally Knitbone really liked the smell – it's a dog's favourite – but this time it was tinged with something unpleasant: a sharp tang of trouble.

"I think you must have licked that aniseed ball to nothing," said Knitbone. "It's very strong, isn't it? The smell, I mean."

Martin carried on reading. "I don't know what you're on about. The aniseed ball is over there next to the joystick. I've barely touched it."

"How strange," murmured Knitbone. "The smell is everywhere."

Martin sat up and sniffed deeply. "Ah, hang on...yes, now I smell it." He smiled, his little white teeth glinting in the moonlight. "Oh! That really does bring back happy memories. William's pockets were always stuffed with those sweets." He threw himself down on his tummy and began reading again. "Now go away and leave me alone."

But instead of leaving, Knitbone's ears pricked up. The hackles rose along his spine as his senses took over and he suddenly sprang into guard-dog mode.

"Oh, honestly – dogs! What's wrong with you lot?" asked Martin indignantly. "Can't a hamster read a comic in peace?"

"Shhh!" Knitbone let out a deep throaty growl. "We are not alone." He bared his teeth. "Who goes there? I know you're here! I can smell you. Come out, whoever you are!" He sniffed the air and snarled. "Come out, I say, or I will come and find you myself! This is your last warning!"

At first nothing happened and everything in the cockpit was very still. But gradually the curtain began to twitch. It jiggled and trembled and slid very slowly across its runners. As it did, a shimmering silvery outline stepped out, phasing in and out, flickering like a film from the olden days. The ghostly figure lifted a leather-gloved hand and gave a smart salute.

"Hello, old chum. Thought I'd pop by." The figure grinned. "Call the guard dog off, would you?"

Martin stood limply, gawping at the ghost before him. He'd had dreams about this happening. He wasn't sure that it was real, so he gave himself a pinch just to be sure. Martin's little mouth flapped open and shut like a letter box in the wind, but no words came out, only a strangled squeak. Eventually he managed to say, "Stand down, Knitbone Pepper, this is no stranger." He stood as straight as his wobbling knees would

allow, gave a little salute and said, "Private Martin Pepper, reporting for duty, sir." Then he dashed across the cabin and clung to William's trouser leg, burying his little face in the fabric.

"Now now, enough of that," said William, bending down to pat Martin. "We'll have no tears. Stiff upper lip and all that. I've been in

a few scrapes since we last met. How long has it been? About seventy years!" He looked up at Knitbone. "And who's this?"

Knitbone tried saluting, with limited success. "My name is Knitbone Pepper."

"Unusual name, fine moustache," said the man. "Splendid to meet you, Knitbone Pepper. William Pepper at your service." He inspected Knitbone's wispy outline, looking him up and down. "Oh, I see – we are all ghosts! Fancy that. And animals that can talk! Is this some sort of ghost club?" He cleared his throat and raised his eyebrow. "Listen here, old thing, I don't mean to be rude, but are you all *animals*? Are there any humans in this ghost club?"

Knitbone wagged his tail, eager to please. "Winnie's human, but she's not a ghost."

"Winnie? Who's she?"

Knitbone stood up very straight, bursting with pride. "Winnie's the cleverest girl in all the

world, of course. She's your granddaughter."
Then Knitbone had a bright idea and, before he'd
had a chance to think about it, he blurted it out.
"Would you like to come into the house and
meet her?"

"Oh yes, William, please come inside and
meet everyone, they'll be so pleased you're
home!" cried Martin, quickly wiping his eyes
with the back of his paw, hoping that nobody
noticed.

"An invitation? Well, my old boots!" William
burst into gales of laughter. "And an audience
you say? Chocks away!"

# Chapter 10

# FREE SPIRIT

William sprang out of the plane and landed on the dewy grass. Martin clung to his shoulder as William strode across the lawn in the moonlight. As Knitbone trotted alongside, trying to keep up, he felt very excited – Martin's special person and Winnie's grandfather was back! William seemed really nice, which was surprising because human ghosts normally spelled TROUBLE in capital letters. He hoped the others would be happy too.

"Excuse me, William," he panted, "but should I let everyone know that you are here first? After all, no one is expecting you, so it's bound to be a bit of a shock."

"But I thought you said this was a ghost club?" said William, who showed no sign of slowing down. "Surely everyone is welcome."

"Actually, *you* said it was a ghost club, not me," said Knitbone, feeling suddenly anxious. He thought of the last human ghost to visit Starcross – the highwayman terror who was Galloping Jasper. He tried to explain. "We're only used to animal spirits at Starcross, you see, and they are quite different."

But William didn't seem to be listening as he bounced energetically up the front steps, taking two at a time. As he got to the top he looked up at the family crest above the door, at the crumbling brickwork and ivy climbing up the wall. "By Jove," he laughed, "the old place hasn't changed a jot! Look," he said pointing to a W inexpertly carved into the stone archway, "I did that with my penknife! Was grounded for a week, ha-ha! Happy days." He barged the heavy oak front door open, stepped over the threshold and tossed his flying hat onto the hall table. "I'm home!" he bellowed. "Anyone in?"

At the top of the stairs, Winnie and the other Beloveds suddenly appeared, looking as startled as a herd of deer.

"WHO on earth are you?" demanded Winnie, alarmed by the intruder. "And what are you doing in my house?"

"Now that's what I like – a girl with spirit!"

But Winnie's blood was up. "I *SAID* –" she unsheathed a savage-looking sword from the display on the wall – "*WHO* ARE YOU AND *WHAT* ARE YOU DOING IN MY HOUSE?"

William took an aniseed ball out of his

pocket, threw it in the air and caught it in his mouth. "Well, actually –" he grinned, rattling the sweet around his teeth – "I think you'll find it's MY house."

"What?"

Gabriel stepped forward and lowered the sword with an outstretched wing. "Winnie, it's alright, we know him. At least, we used to."

Winnie squinted and noticed William's wispy edges in amazement. "But…but you're a ghost!"

"YES, he is!" Martin stood up on William's shoulder. "Oh, Winnie, Winnie! The most wonderful thing has happened!" he cried in delight. "I want to introduce you to William Pepper – *my* special person and *your* grandfather! He's come home and now we can be together for ever at last! Isn't it absolutely the best news?"

Winnie slumped down onto the top step in shock. "Of course. I recognize you now, you're in the box of photos," she murmured.

"Smart for a girl, eh?" William tapped his temple and winked. "Glad to see you've inherited my brains."

Winnie frowned. "But there are rules – we only have animal ghosts at Starcross. We don't have human ghosts."

William helped himself to a ginger biscuit from the table, expertly tossing it into his mouth and swallowing it in one gulp. "Well, you've jolly well got one *now*! Ha-ha!"

"Isn't it marvellous, Winnie?" Martin's eyes shone with happiness and wonder, as he slid down the length of William's flying jacket and did a little dance on the spot. "He's back and now we'll be best friends again, just like you and Knitbone! I've never been happier in my whole life or death than at this *very moment*."

William elbowed past Winnie and the Beloveds and loped up the stairs, Martin scampering after him. "I must say I'm pooped," yawned William. "Time for lights out soon, I think. Dorm inspection first, though." He strode down the corridor and pushed open Winnie's bedroom door.

"Where do you think you're going?" exclaimed Winnie, chasing after him.

William looked around the room, at the wardrobe, the bed, the bookshelves. "Barely changed at all. Good work, Private Martin! Just look at these scrapbooks. But these will have to go, of course," he said, taking down Winnie's posters. "We need pictures of bazookas, spitfires and tanks, not soppy plants and planets." Then William threw himself on the patchwork quilt, boots and all, and immediately fell into a deep sleep. Martin scrambled up and lay down next to him. He closed his eyes and they both began to snore like wasps in a jar.

Winnie stood in the doorway, arms crossed, teeth gritted and brow knitted. "Somebody had

better have a good explanation for this."
Knitbone's tail drooped and he retreated beneath
the landing table.

Gabriel gestured to the attic. "I think it's time
for an S.O.S. meeting."

"WHO DOES HE THINK HE IS?" asked
Winnie, stomping into the attic in a temper,
posters rolled up under her arm. "He can't just
turn up. That's MY bedroom. It may have been
his seventy years ago but it's not now!" She
unravelled a sleeping bag and lay it out on the
hard wooden floor. "And he pongs of aniseed
balls. I thought Martin said he was great?"

Knitbone saw the determined look in her eyes
and the stubborn set of her jaw. It was clear that
William had really rubbed Winnie up the wrong
way, but he couldn't help thinking that they had
more in common than she might like to admit.
He decided that now was probably not the time
to mention it.

"William is stinky man," said Orlando, pegging his nose. He retched, like a cat throwing up a furball.

"Oh, come on," said Valentine, writing *Spirits of Starcross Emergency Meeting* on the blackboard. "Mind your manners, please. Don't forget William is Martin's special person. He is

Starcross home-grown family and he belongs
here as much as we do. He's just going to take
a bit of getting used to, that's all."

"But you know what human ghosts are like!
Remember Galloping Jasper? How badly he

treated Moon?" Winnie pulled down *The Good Ghost Guide* and began to quote from it: "'*Human ghosts are famous show-offs, always going on about themselves.*' Relative or not, why would we want one in the house? How did he get in? William must have been trapped in *The Silver Phantom* for all those years. "

The smell of peppermint filled the air, a dead giveaway that there was an embarrassed Beloved nearby. Knitbone shuffled his paws awkwardly. "Um…it was me. I invited him into the house."

"Oh, Knitbone!" Winnie looked disappointed and it was more than Knitbone could bear.

"But…but," whimpered Knitbone. "Martin was happy again and I thought it would all be alright. I just want everyone to be happy."

Gabriel flicked through *The Good Ghost Guide* until he found the relevant page. "Ah, just as I thought. Unfortunately an official invitation by a Spirit of Starcross means we can't make him leave – he'll have to leave the estate of his own free will."

"So we're stuck with him? But he's stolen my bedroom!" wailed Winnie. Knitbone buried his nose in his paws and let out a long whine.

"There there," said Winnie, sighing deeply and stroking his ears. "Don't worry. You were only doing what you thought right. We'll just have to make the best of it." She pinned her astronomy and botanical posters up on the attic wall and climbed into the sleeping bag, zipping it up to her chin.

"Well, I really don't know what you're all making such a fuss about," yawned Valentine, settling down to sleep on the attic floor. "William's a bit of a scallywag, that's all. You'll get used to him. Do you remember all those pranks he and Martin used to get up to, eh, Gabriel? It'll be fun!"

## Chapter 11

# PRANKS AND PEPPERWHACKERS

The next morning, just before sunrise, Valentine became aware of a tickling sensation in his sleep. He was having the most lovely dream about lying in a flower-filled meadow. The sun was shining, gently warming his fur, as a peacock butterfly landed right on the tip on his nose. He flared his nostrils and twitched his ears – what a beautiful afternoon. But then, suddenly, the butterfly in his dream became an angry mosquito! Panicked, Valentine swatted at his nose with his paw – SPLAT!

Valentine snapped awake, sat up and opened his eyes. He looked down in confusion to see that his face was dripping with yellow-something. He licked his nose – it tasted sweet.

William and Martin were rolling about the attic floor, helpless with laughter. Martin was brandishing a feather duster and William held a tin of custard.

"OH! We got you!" gasped William, clutching his sides. "The old sleepy tickler trick! Put a dish of custard in the hand and give the nose a little tickle – wham! Gets 'em every time!"

"Oh, William," giggled Martin, who now seemed to have a little waxed moustache just like his hero. "You're SO funny. Isn't he funny, everyone?"

"Oh, yes," fumed Valentine, as Orlando lovingly licked all the custard from his face. "William's *hilarious* alright."

William sprang to his feet and put his hands on his hips. "Right, what's the morning drill round here, eh?"

Winnie sat up in her sleeping bag. "*The drill?* We don't have a drill." She looked blearily at her pocket watch. "It's only 5.30 a.m. It's a bit early, isn't it?"

"Nonsense. We've been up for hours. Come on, Martin, early bird catches the worm."

William exited the attic, Martin skipping behind him. Knitbone stretched out his back legs, then his front ones and yawned. He looked sheepishly up at Winnie. "At least Martin seems to be in a cheerful mood now," he said.

"Yes," said Winnie doubtfully. "At least that's something, I suppose."

"Come on," said Gabriel, clambering to his feet. "We'd better go and see what they're up to."

Lord and Lady Pepper were already awake, stumbling around the kitchen looking exhausted. Lady Pepper still had her sleeping mask on her head. For once Lord Pepper was hatless.

"You look as if you haven't slept a wink," said Winnie, helping herself to a slice of turnip toast and conker marmalade. Winnie munched and munched, spotting the black-and-white photograph of William and Martin propped up next to the butter dish. She turned and noticed her father's red-rimmed eyes and pink-tipped nose in alarm. "Daddy, have you been crying?"

"Most certainly not!" sniffled Lord Pepper, blowing his nose loudly. "Lords don't cry. This news about my long-lost father just came as a bit of a surprise, that's all." He stuffed his hanky back into his pocket. "You see, I was always told he was on a very long holiday and would be back one day, but now that dream has been dashed."

Lady Pepper poured a cup of steaming beetroot tea into Lord Pepper's china cup and rested her hand on his shoulder. "I'm sure that if he'd had the chance to get to know you, he would have been very proud of you, dear."

"If only he'd been around while I was growing up," sniffed Lord Pepper. "Grandpa died when I was four, so when I came home from boarding school in the holidays there was no one here but the servants. It was rather gloomy at Starcross for a long time, with just the hats to play with." He looked up at his wife and beamed. "But then you

and Winnie came into my life and the sunshine poured in." Lady Pepper smiled and patted his shoulder.

"And on the bright side," continued Lord Pepper, cheering up, "I bet my father was a smashing chap. He was probably on some super-secret mission when *The Silver Phantom* crashed."

"Smashing?" coughed Winnie, thinking about the prankster who had taken over her bedroom. She took a savage bite out of her toast. "How do you know?"

"When I was at boarding school – St Charity's Institution for the Posh 'n' Poor – he was all the teachers ever talked about," said Lord Pepper. "William was a school legend. He was a bit of a scamp – they had a cane named after him: the Pepperwhacker. They kept it in a display case above the doorway as a warning to rebels." Lord Pepper lowered his eyes and fiddled with his dressing-gown tassel. "Of course, I was shy and only interested in hats."

Lady Pepper patted his shoulder. "There, there, Hector, you are a fine and good man."

Lord Pepper rose to his feet. "Yes, dear, but my father was a *real* hero. As a young man he was a flying ace in the Royal Air Force." He pointed to a medal pinned to his pyjamas. "This is the Air Force Cross, awarded for valour, courage and bravery. It will be an honour to do the interview in his memory."

Winnie looked up from her tea in surprise. "Interview? What interview?"

"With Penny Farthing for *Junk Palace,* of course," said Lady Pepper, putting the tea cosy on the teapot. "Today they are just doing lots of shots around the house but tomorrow she wants to do an extra feature on William – *your* grandfather – for the show."

Lord Pepper looked into the middle distance, misty-eyed. "A fitting tribute to my noble, dearly-departed father that will be broadcast worldwide."

"That clever Hattie person says that she's found out all sorts of things about your grandfather that will amaze us," said Lady Pepper, "and I for one can't wait. She says she's going to spend today searching for more facts – in the library, the ballroom – everywhere! Who knows what will turn up?"

"Are you sure this is a good idea?" asked Winnie, glancing anxiously down at Knitbone, who lay beneath the kitchen table with the others. "Maybe it's best to let sleeping dogs lie…" They were interrupted by a sudden loud crash. Winnie leaped up and ran out into the hallway.

"Don't worry, dear," Lord Pepper called after her, dipping his nettle crumpet into the honey jar. "It's probably just the owls doing laps around the house again!"

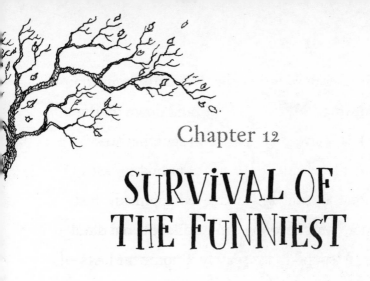

## Chapter 12

# SURVIVAL OF THE FUNNIEST

O f course it wasn't owls causing the terrible racket – it was William and Martin larking about. They lay sprawled in a giggling ghostly heap at the bottom of the stairs, a dented antique silver tray lying next to them. Knitbone noticed that William's pockets were stuffed with pink wafers.

"Not bad, Martin, not bad at all," laughed William. "We slid down those stairs like greased lightning, eh? That old tray makes a brilliant sledge."

Martin jumped up and down on the spot, his eyes twinkling with happiness. "Just like the old days! Ripping fun! Again! Again!"

Winnie picked up the tray and decided not to mention the big dent in her mother's best silver.

"Winnie!" Martin grinned, looking up. "There you are! I was just telling William how much fun we have at Starcross. Do you think you could come and play with us today? I thought we could build go-carts! William's brilliant at building things."

Knitbone wagged his tail hopefully. "Oh, can we, Winnie? Can we?" he woofed. "I love a race!"

"Oh, yes!" chorused the gang. "That sounds like fun!"

Winnie looked at everyone's hopeful faces and wondered if she was being unfair about William. Maybe Valentine, Martin and her father were right – William was just a bit of a scamp. "Come on, then." She smiled, reaching down to help William up. "Let's go and have some proper old-fashioned Starcross fun."

Behind the house stood an old, abandoned air-raid shelter, built from sheets of rusty corrugated iron and nestled in a forest of nettles. It was large and over the years had been stuffed with junk. It was a treasure trove of old wheelbarrows, bikes, packing cases, chains and general farm scrap – it was a go-cart builder's dream.

The teams spent a busy morning drawing up technical plans and choosing interesting parts. They hammered, screwed, bashed and lashed

together parts until, eventually, two magnificent
vehicles stood side by side on the brow of the
hill, looking down over Starcross Hall.

Wearing matching flying goggles, Martin
and William stood by their go-cart, a vehicle
constructed from a pram, a vacuum cleaner and

a clothes horse. By the other go-cart stood
Winnie and Knitbone. Their machine was built
from a lawnmower, some bedsprings and
Knitbone's old kennel. As she was the only one at
risk of getting hurt, it was decided that Winnie
should wear a saucepan helmet.

Gabriel pulled out a clipboard. "What are the names of your go-carts, please?"

"Ours is called *The Starcross Rocket*," said Knitbone.

"William says to call ours *The Winner*," said Martin.

"Right! Ready, steady…" Valentine slashed a sandcastle flag down through the air. "*GO!*"

Knitbone and Martin sprang into their front seats. William and Winnie ran at the rear, shoving as hard as they could to build up speed before diving in at the last moment. The two go-carts flew down the hill, neck and neck, shuddering and juddering, teeth rattling, springs, bolts and screws pinging off as they went. Winnie and Knitbone lowered their heads into the wind, plaits and floppy ears flying, focused on the finishing line.

But out of the blue – *SMASH!* – William steered hard to the right and crashed into *The Starcross Rocket,* forcing it to skid sideways. Suddenly *The Winner* hit a bump in the grass, sending William and Martin high up into the air. "Tally-ho!" squealed Martin, clinging tightly to William's flying hat as they crash-landed in a spiky patch of brambles.

"William! That's cheating," shouted Winnie, pulling off her saucepan hat crossly. "It was supposed to be a race, not a war!"

William laughed loudly as he pulled the brambles out of his jacket. "If there's no danger, where is the fun? What shall we play now?" He looked about and noticed a pile of old crockery stacked up at the side of a barn. With a mad glint in his eye, he reached into his pocket and took out a catapult. "I know, let's SMASH STUFF!"

After reducing the plates and cups to a large pile of china splinters, he insisted they all play "loudest burp", welly-wanging and tree-swing battles. They played tag, British bulldog, marbles, skipping, hopscotch, leapfrog, cartwheels and cross-country running. They had three games of football, played musical chairs, hurdled over gates and had piggyback races.

While the Beloveds lay gasping on the floor, William, still full of energy, clambered up trees and sang rude songs from the top branches.

He threw stones at the crows, causing them to scatter into the sky like off-key musical notes. To top it off he made a Stonking Stink that was *so bad* a nearby family of rabbits were forced underground. This went on until the sun went down and it was too dark to see.

"Didn't I say so, everyone?" said Martin, panting between yawns and whimpers as they limped back in the dark. "Didn't I say that William was brilliant fun? The life and soul of the party? He's the best friend a Beloved could have and I hope he stays at Starcross for ever and ever. And now I bet you love him too!"

But by now the other Beloveds were pretty sure they *didn't* love William. A worrying thought kept popping up in Knitbone's brain.

The previous day, William must have known that Martin had been sitting in *The Silver Phantom* all afternoon feeling sad, so why hadn't he come out before? If he still cared about Martin, why did he only come out from behind the curtain when Knitbone threatened him? That didn't seem like the sort of thing a friend would do, never mind a hero.

One thing was for sure: his animal instinct told him that Martin was in trouble. He thought of the warning in *The Good Ghost Guide*: *Human ghosts are famous show-offs, always going on about themselves.* William was definitely a selfish show-off. But the little hamster seemed so happy to be reunited with his friend at long last, Knitbone lowered his gaze and just wagged his tail half-heartedly instead.

# Chapter 13

# PARTY POOPER

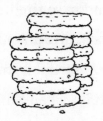

That night Winnie was shaken from a deep sleep by Martin tugging at her pyjamas. "Wake up! Wake up, everybody, William's got *another* brilliant idea. He says we should have a midnight feast!"

"A what?" said Knitbone groggily, lying at Winnie's feet.

"A feast?" protested Gabriel, looking up at the moon through the attic window. "But it's the middle of the night."

"That's the whole point," hissed Martin, brushing pink crumbs from his face. "It couldn't be a midnight feast in the middle of the *day*, could it? Come on, we've got loads of biscuits and some party games lined up."

"But I'm so tired…" Knitbone grumbled.

"Oh PLEASE, Knitbone," begged Martin. "William really wants to and I don't want to let him down." His little hamster eyes looked desperate. "*Please.*"

The gang all stumbled sleepily down the attic stairs to Winnie's bedroom. Gabriel muttered to Valentine behind his wing, "I don't get it. Why isn't William tired yet? I'm worn out after today's malarkey."

"He's always stuffing pink wafers," said Valentine. "I bet that's got something to do with it. Martin is too."

As they got to the bedroom door they could hear voices – new voices. Winnie stopped dead in her tracks and her eyes widened in alarm. "Is there someone else in there? Who's that?" she hissed at Martin. "I thought it was just the two of you!"

"Ah. Yes," said Martin. "I was just going to tell you about that bit…"

William flung the door open, grinning broadly and wearing a paper crown. "Ah, you're here! Perfect timing. Come in, come in, join the party! Surprise!" He tooted on a little party blower, bopping Winnie on the nose.

Knitbone peered around the door frame. He instantly stood to attention, his tail pointing straight up and trembling. "WHO," he growled, "are *they*?"

Three wispy strangers had appeared in Winnie's bedroom. Two of them had biscuits raised halfway to their mouths and looked up in surprise. The other was on his knees, inspecting the floorboards.

"Of course, how rude of me, I haven't introduced you to everyone," said William. "What a terrible host I am. This", he said, pointing to a tall, sour-faced old woman, "is the Edwardian governess Euphemia Fork." Euphemia looked down her nose at the Beloveds and turned away with a haughty sniff. "This", continued William, "is Sick Billy the Victorian stable boy, and that one over there is Finias the butler." William pointed at the whiskery old man,

who was still scrabbling at the floorboards.
He seemed to be trying to pull them up, picking
at the nails and mumbling away to himself.

"But why is he doing that? Could you just *stop*
him doing that, please? What is he doing to my
floorboards? I need a bedroom floor!" Winnie
closed her eyes in exasperation and tried to
breathe deeply. "William, am I correct
in thinking that your party guests
are *ghosts*?"

"Of course!" chuckled William, sucking an aniseed ball. "What else would they be?"

"Oh YES, Euphemia, Billy and Finias!" marvelled Valentine. "I remember them now. Do you, Gabriel?"

Gabriel nodded in amazement, his eyes fixed on the visitors. "I remember when they were *alive*," he whispered, "but I've never seen them dead before, or any *human* Starcross ghosts, for that matter. I've only ever met animal ghosts here. Where have they suddenly sprung from?"

It was then that they noticed *The Good Ghost Guide* lying wide open on the rug.

"Oh dear. Oh no," said Gabriel quietly, looking alarmed. "That is supposed to be hidden in the library."

"I couldn't sleep," explained William. "I was desperately trying to find something interesting to do around here. In fact, I was

SO BORED I told Martin that I would probably leave. But then he showed me the book."

There was a long, awkward silence while Winnie and the Beloveds glared at Martin, who merely shrugged his furry shoulders. "So what?" he muttered. "Gabriel is always saying how important books are. Cheer up, William's part of our gang too, isn't he? Why shouldn't he see the book? It's only fair, to my mind."

He let off a party popper, hoping it would lighten the mood. It didn't.

Meanwhile, William flicked through the pages of *The Good Ghost Guide*. "Now *normally*, other than comics, I'm not much of a reader, but this book is a real page-turner. There are some stupid bits, like where it says that human ghosts are 'show-offs', but there was interesting stuff too. Look!" He held it up so they could all read the words:

Human ghosts can only be woken by other human ghosts.

"What do you think about that? Sounds like fun, doesn't it? *I'm* a human ghost so I thought I'd invite a few more jolly souls along for the ride, spice things up a bit. Only thing is, it doesn't give any instructions, so I just did what any party host would do and posted a general invitation." He pointed up to Winnie's chalkboard on the back of the door.

Human spirits
You are invited to a party
to wake the dead
MIDNIGHT
TONIGHT
All welcome!

William looked gloomily over at the cross old woman, the pale boy and the floorboard scrabbler. "But they were the only ones to turn up. Party poopers, the lot of them. But I'm just a beginner," he said. "Next time I think my party will be much more popular."

"NEXT TIME?" chorused the Beloveds in horror.

"Well, of course!" laughed William, as if he was stating the most obvious thing in the world.

"It'll be better with human ghosts around the old place. After all, you can't really expect me to be happy with just animals for company, can you?"

Martin looked sad and stared hard at his feet. Knitbone wanted to give him a hug.

Winnie pointed her finger at William. "I know this might seem funny to you, but you're playing with fire. You're messing with something you don't understand. It's NOT a game."

William rolled his eyes. "This isn't a problem, it's an opportunity."

"What do you mean?" asked Gabriel.

"He means," said Martin, looking up at Orlando, Gabriel and Valentine, "something amazing!" He lifted his arms up to the sky. "He *means* that he can fulfil your heart's desire: he can call your special people back!"

There was a long, shocked silence as the Beloveds took the enormity of this in.

Orlando didn't need telling twice. He crept

towards William, his knees wobbly. "Please, Mister William, can you please-thank-you bring my Lovelace back?" begged Orlando, his eyes big and round. "Lovelace Pepper? To feed me 'lishous custard from her special silver-necklace spoon? Have you seen her? She has shiny soft hair and smells of happy."

Valentine hopped over to Euphemia, his ears standing up in hope. "Pardon me, madam, but I don't suppose you've seen my best friend, Elrick the Brave, back there, have you? Wears a lot of shiny armour? Carries a lance? Because I've not seen him in over eight hundred years and I...I miss him." He turned to William with a desperate smile. "If you could bring him back for even just five minutes that would be enough."

"No, wait," said Knitbone, leafing frantically through the pages of the book. "This is very dangerous. I've read about it somewhere...look!" He pointed his paw at the page.

*Human ghosts and their Beloveds*
*Do Not Mix*

Reuniting a Beloved with
the **ghost** of their special
person is **high risk**.

**Danger of disappointment
and/or oblivion.**

But Gabriel was beyond listening. He craned
his neck up towards William. "My person's name
is Winstanley Pepper," said Gabriel. "Spelled
W-I-N-S-T-A-N-L-E-Y." His beak began to wobble
uncontrollably and his honk became high-
pitched. "Could you bring back Winstanley?
I last saw him in 1674 but he was very old. He
went out to the market and never came back.

I...I know he'd like to see what I've done with the library. I think he'd be proud of me. I miss him so much, you see."

Orlando, Valentine and Gabriel looked as if they were in a lovelorn trance, gazing up at William, lost in a desperate hope that they might meet their people once more.

Winnie clapped her hands to get their attention. "This is terrible – snap out of it, everyone! What are you saying?" she cried. "You heard Knitbone, it's too dangerous!"

"Oh, Winnie," said Martin, "don't be such a fusspot. William says that rules are made to be broken. Look at me! I'm perfectly fine, aren't I?"

"I don't know about that, Martin," growled Knitbone. "I'm not at all sure you *are* perfectly fine. Ever since *The Silver Phantom* arrived and William turned up, you've not been yourself at all. It's far too risky if you ask me."

William barged between them, knocking

Martin sideways. "But no one IS asking you, Knitbone Pepper, are they? It's their choice, they can do what they want," he said, a mischievous twinkle in his eye. "Don't be such a sissy."

Winnie shook her head in disgust and put her arm around Knitbone, whose fur was now standing on end. "You *may* be the grown-up round here, William Pepper, but you should be ashamed of yourself."

William waved his hand in a bored manner. "Listen, I'm only giving the rabbit and the duck and that strange little monkey what they want, aren't I? At least I'm helping, not like you."

Winnie locked eyes with William. Once again Knitbone was struck by the family resemblance; by the fire in their glares, the stubborn set of their jaws.

Winnie stood on tiptoe, her face red with fury. "Listen to me, William Pepper. Ever since you arrived you've caused nothing but trouble. I WILL NOT let you hurt my friends. We were happy before you came along. We're a gang, we're family. You think you're so clever, but I bet you don't even know what Oblivion means, do you?"

William shrugged and tossed another pink wafer into his mouth. "No, but I have a feeling you're going to tell me."

Knitbone turned to the correct page and read it out loud.

# Beloved Oblivion

Symptom Checker: A sensation of melting like a snowflake on the tongue.

Duration: Seventeen seconds.

Progression: Disappearance of body until all that remains is a faint echo of laughter in the brickwork.

Cure: There isn't one.

Possible Causes: A) Attempting to cross home boundaries or
B) Deliberately and recklessly reuniting with human <u>ghost</u>

<u>Pain Level: No one has survived to say.</u>

"Excuse me interrupting," said Euphemia Fork, raising her hand and pursing her lemon-sucker lips. She pointed at the ghost of the mumbly old butler, who was still trying to prise up the floorboards. "Finias is trying to say something."

But now it was William's turn to be in a temper. "I know! I know! He's told me. In fact he hasn't shut up about it since he arrived!" William turned on Winnie, shutting out Euphemia. "Listen, granddaughter of mine, you don't have any idea what it's like to be dead. It's alright for you, swanning about in the real world. If ONLY that lightning storm hadn't struck, if ONLY I'd remembered to check my parachute," he ranted. "Well, it could have happened to anyone. The point is I'd give my right propeller to be alive again, cruising the skies, seeking adventure. I must say I'm getting rather tired of you and your *opinions*."

"YEAH," said Martin, hitching up his utility belt. "You tell her, William. She's a right Minnie-moaner and know-it-all."

Martin had gone too far and Knitbone leaped to Winnie's defence. He fixed Martin with a steely glare and growled very deeply. "Don't you

EVER speak to Winnie like that or…"

Martin held his sword right next to Knitbone's nose. "OR WHAT? Go on, I dares you, you…you mongrel!"

"That's it, Martin," laughed William, enjoying the scene he was causing. Knitbone noticed he seemed more vivid than ever, his edges hardly wispy at all. "Show him who's the boss around here!"

"Stop it, stop it!" honked Gabriel, finally coming to his senses. He flapped his wings and waddled around in a circle, looking very distressed. "We're supposed to be best friends. This is awful-awful-awful!"

"This is absolutely the worst party I've ever been to," huffed Winnie, slamming the book shut. "And now it's over."

"YOU are just a CHILD!" raged William. "You can't tell me what to do!"

Winnie rallied, her temper flaring. "Yes I can,

because this is MY house, I live here and, as you pointed out, I'm the only one here who is ACTUALLY ALIVE. That's it, you can sleep in your plane from now on. I've had enough of you." She pointed her finger at him and narrowed her eyes. "You're not just any old fun-loving prankster, *you're a bad spirit, William Pepper*. GET OUT AND TAKE YOUR RUBBISH PARTY GHOSTS WITH YOU!"

"Well I shall!" he bellowed back. "I was leaving anyway!" William stomped down the stairway and out into the cold night.

Through the bedroom window they watched him storm across the courtyard by moonlight, Martin running to keep up, balancing a tower of pink wafers in his arms.

"I tried to like William because he was Martin's friend," said Knitbone, his nose pressed to the window and his temper ebbing away. "I tried really hard, but it's not easy, is it?"

Winnie gave Knitbone a hug. "That
grandfather of mine is a nightmare alright."

"Sorry-sorry-sorry," gabbled Gabriel, looking
embarrassed and gesturing to Orlando and
Valentine. The smell of peppermint blushes in
Winnie's bedroom was quite overwhelming. "We
went a bit doolally there for a moment. Of course

it's dangerous to bring our people back, it's why we've never tried it before. But William made it sound so easy."

"But we don't want to disappear like snowflakes, do we?" asked Valentine, putting his arms around the others. "Even if it does mean meeting our special people again."

"No," said Gabriel. "We might be dead, but there's still too much to live for."

"There's monkey business to get up to." Orlando folded his arms tightly across his chest. "Silly to be drippy lolly in the walls."

The bedroom was under Winnie's control again and everyone settled down in their usual places, right at the end of the bed. Unfortunately William had neglected to collect his human ghosts, so they hung about in the corner, looking at each other, not sure what to do next. Then, when it was all becoming unbearably awkward, Euphemia, Sick Billy and Finias faded away, much to everyone's relief.

Exhausted by the night's shenanigans,
Knitbone curled up on Winnie's feet and
Valentine stretched his long body alongside.
Gabriel snuggled up too, his head under his
wing. Orlando lay right on top of the pile,
hugging a spoon to his heart.

But there was an empty space beneath
Knitbone's chin where Martin normally slept.
Without him there the whole pile felt wrong and
in the end nobody got a wink of sleep.

## Chapter 14

# UNQUIET SPIRIT

The morning after the terrible party row,
everyone was fed up. There had been a lot
of tossing and turning in Winnie's creaky bed and
everyone was in a bit of a grump.

Winnie pulled on her clothes and trudged out
of her bedroom, bumping into Hattie on her way
down the corridor. "Oh, hello, Hattie," said
Winnie in surprise. "What are you doing here?
Can I help you with something?"

Hattie looked startled. "Oh, er…I was just

looking for the…um…bathroom. Yes, that's it.
Is it along here?"

Winnie nodded absent-mindedly. "It's just
down there on the left," she said, "but watch out
for the bats – they've moved into the airing
cupboard now."

As Winnie and the Beloveds plodded down the stairs in single file they spotted Mrs Jones waiting for them on the rim of her vase. Knitbone growled – that was all they needed. She held up her front legs in a fake gesture of joy, as if to celebrate their arrival.

"Well, well," she said, "if it isn't the bumbling Beloveds."

Mrs Jones was a Bad Egg, an ill-wind and a pain in the neck. Her appearance never heralded good news.

"What do *you* want?" said Knitbone.

"Tut tut. Well *that's* not very friendly, Knickerface Pickle, is it?" She clacked her fangs with glee and her eight eyes sparkled spitefully. "I was only wondering if you'd like to take part in a quiz."

"A quiz?" Knitbone raised an eyebrow. "What's the catch?"

"No catch. It's just that if you get the answer wrong I shall win all of the ginger biscuits in your secret cupboard upstairs. BUT if you get the answer right I'll tell you something funny about Martin's *special friend*. I've been watching him with great interest."

"I'm not in the mood for your nonsense this morning, Mrs Jones," grumbled Knitbone. "So the answer is no."

"I see," she said. "I forgot that you lot are thicker than cold porridge. You're probably not clever enough anyway..." Mrs Jones began to slide backwards into her vase.

"Stop!" honked Gabriel, turning to Knitbone. "She might be mean but she's also nosy. She might know something we don't. Ask *me* the question, Mrs Jones."

"Oh, goody-goody!" Mrs Jones pulled herself

back onto the rim and clacked her fangs in anticipation. "Ginger biscuits here I come!" She cleared her throat and then, in vinegary tones, she began.

*"My first is in thunder that comes from afar,*
*my second is the spirit of who we are.*

"Right," she snapped. "What's the answer? Come on, quickly now. You have sixteen seconds to get it right and then the biscuits are mine. Agreed? Yes? Good. One…two…three…"

Gabriel was thinking very hard. "Knitbone," he said, "write this down." Knitbone picked up a pencil with his teeth and held it poised over the telephone notepad.

"Seven…eight…nine…"

*"My first is in thunder*… I think that must be *rumble*." Gabriel waddled around the hallway deep in thought.

"Twelvethirteenfourteen…" Suddenly nervous, Mrs Jones began to speed up.

"And I think the second – *the spirit of who we are* – must be *ghost*." Gabriel's eyes widened in delight. "I've got it! The answer is RUMBLEGHOST!"

Mrs Jones was absolutely furious and fell backwards into the vase. "CHEAT!" she screeched from the bottom. "Rotten cheats! I don't know how you cheated but I bet you did! Those biscuits are mine fair and square. I know a bad 'un when I see one!" Winnie placed a saucer on top of the vase to muffle her protest.

Knitbone looked down at the piece of paper and shook his head. "I'm sorry, I still don't understand. What's a *rumbleghost* and what's it got to do with William?"

"There's a whole chapter on them in the

book," said Valentine. "A rumbleghost is an unquiet spirit."

Knitbone looked up blankly. Gabriel honked and flapped his wings. "A rumbleghost is also known as a *poltergeist*! They are the most troublesome of all ghosts, causing chaos wherever they go, feeding off bad feelings."

"Of course! So *that's* why William's so exhausting!" cried Winnie. "It's not the pink wafers at all – it's us arguing, isn't it?! It's making him stronger! I *said* he was a bad spirit, didn't I? I *knew* it right from the start."

"Eez big podlob," said Orlando, climbing onto Knitbone's head.

"William is a picklechops."

"Imagine being best friends

with a rumbleghost," said Winnie. "Poor Martin, what a nightmare. Well, we'll just have to tell him. Then he can explain to William he can't be his friend any more, William will leave of his own accord and everything at Starcross will be happy again." Winnie swung around the stair banister and spun off towards the kitchen.

Knitbone turned and cast a doom-laden glance at the others, his tail drooping low. If only it were that simple. They all knew that Martin, a true and devoted Beloved, would most likely go to the ends of the earth for William.

# Chapter 15

# HAPLESS HISTORY

Knitbone and the gang followed Winnie into the deserted kitchen, Orlando still balancing on the dog's head. "I wonder where Lord and Lady P are?" said Knitbone, sniffing the teapot. "They're normally still eating breakfast about now."

Gabriel craned his long neck and looked out of the window and honked the alarm: "Visitors ahoy!"

Winnie and the Beloveds looked through the dusty windows to see two more *Junk Palace* vans had arrived in the courtyard. These were very large, rather like removal lorries. "OH! Of course, it's day three, isn't it?" breathed Winnie. "*That's* why Hattie is here! That must be all the filming equipment for Dad's interview. I'd forgotten all about it. I hope we haven't slept through it. Come on!"

Lord and Lady Pepper sat patiently in the library, the blazing studio lights making their faces sweat.

They'd been asked to dress appropriately as it was a serious historical interview. The TV company had brought in a pair of *Junk Palace* branded thrones for them to sit on and placed a large black-and-white photograph of William in his RAF uniform on the table. With his perfect moustache and twinkling eyes, William looked every inch the hero.

Hattie was now standing behind the cameras, checking the library books one by one.

Penny Farthing, meanwhile, was having her make-up finished. She was wearing silk everything – blouse, trousers and scarf. She was so smooth she looked in danger of slipping off her chair.

In contrast, the Peppers were dressed in matching tweed suits and itching like dogs with fleas.

Penny waved away the make-up lady, nodded at the director and cleared her throat.

"So, Lord Hector Pepper," asked Penny smoothly, "let's begin with you telling us a little about your father, William."

"Well, Penny," said Lord Pepper, his voice trembling slightly, "as you know I was just a tiny baby when he disappeared."

Penny put on a sympathetic face, leaned forward and put her hand on his. "This must be very difficult for you."

"Well yes, thank you, it is. I was told by my grandfather's servant, Finias, that William had gone on a very long holiday but would be back one day. Therefore the news that he was killed in a plane crash over fifty years ago has come as a shock. *The Silver Phantom* has put me in something of a tizz."

Penny stopped the filming for a moment and handed him a tissue.

Lord Pepper blew his nose like a trumpet.

"Poor Lord P," whined Knitbone. "This is quite sad. I'm starting to wish *Junk Palace* had never heard of Starcross."

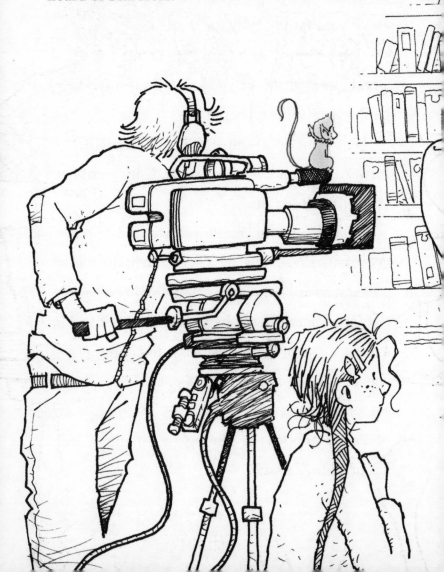

"There's Martin," said Gabriel. Martin was sitting high up on the bookshelves, wedged between Cookery and History. "Should we tell him about William now?"

"Yes, I think we'd better," said Valentine with a sigh. "Come on." They crossed the room and looked up.

"Morning, Martin," woofed Knitbone. "Will you be coming home soon? It's not the same without you. Where's William?"

"He's in *The Silver Phantom*, of course," snapped Martin, "thinking about important things. I'm under orders to watch the interview and take notes."

"Like a seccerterry lady?" asked Orlando.

"NO," protested Martin. "NOT like a secretary lady actually. I'm on a secret mission. I'm more like a super-sleuth spy...or-or-or...a military biographer or an army intelligence officer. William needs me."

Valentine took the plunge. "Are you sure about that? Have you thought that William might be..." Valentine paused and looked sideways at the others for support... "a bad influence?"

"*A bad influence?*" snapped Martin. "What do you mean? He's my hero! Once upon a time he was the most wonderful, generous boy in the world, but just because he's a human ghost now you won't give him a chance, will you?" A furious tear appeared in his eye. "Anyway, I'm going to write my own special account of William's daredevil adventures. Did you know he was charged by a rhino in the Congo? Or that he fought a crocodile in India? I bet you didn't know he saved a whole Russian village from burning down, did you? Or that he had tea with King Kong? No? I didn't *think* so," said Martin, a note of triumph in his tone. "Anyway, I can't be gossiping with the likes of you, listening to silly nonsense about my good friend William. I've got a job to do and, if you don't mind," he said, shuffling his papers in an efficient manner, "I'm extremely busy."

The Beloveds looked at each other, lost for words. Maybe now *wasn't* a good time to mention the rumbleghost problem.

"Shh," said Winnie, noticing the cameras

were rolling again, "Dad's about to say something." Hattie the researcher stood on the other side of the room, a pile of papers in her arms. Winnie smiled and waved but Hattie didn't notice, her eyes firmly fixed on Lord Pepper.

"One thing I would like to say, Penny," said Lord Pepper, sitting up straight, "is that although I don't remember meeting him in person, I am very proud to be his son."

"I see," said Penny, looking at the photograph. She hesitated and nibbled at her pen top. "Would you agree that he was a risk-taker? A bit of a bad boy, maybe?"

"What do you mean?"

"You know, at his boarding school for example? His report says he was expelled for setting fire to the PE shed. Is this true?" She took out an old cane and handed it to Lord Pepper. "And what of this? The legendary Pepperwhacker?"

"Well, yes," said Lord Pepper, "but it was nothing more than high jinks, I'm sure. He was more of a scallywag than a rebel."

Penny looked down at her notes and frowned. "Your daughter is a bit of a rebel too though, isn't she? Maybe being a trouble-magnet runs in the family? All that business with Krispin O'Mystery and the council? Magpie McCracken the international jewel thief? Didn't she cause the renowned astronomer Rosabel Starr to abandon her post at the University of the North Pole?"

The Peppers – both dead *and* alive – looked shocked. "How do you know about that?" asked Lady Pepper.

"How does she know about that?" echoed Knitbone, looking at the others.

Penny moved on. "Our records are very revealing. They show that William did indeed join the Royal Air Force, earned his wings and trained to be a top daredevil pilot. Everything seemed to go well for a few years. It seems he even won the AFC – the Air Force Cross, awarded for valour."

"Oh, yes." Lord Pepper smiled, pleased that the interview seemed to be getting back on track. He tinkled the medal on his jacket. "I have it right here."

"But William couldn't stay out of trouble for long," continued Penny. "Which is why he was *dishonourably discharged from the RAF in 1964*, one year before he mysteriously disappeared for ever!"

Lord Pepper gasped as if he'd been slapped around the face with a wet fish.

Watching the drama unfold from the high shelf, Martin looked flustered. "That can't be right," he muttered to himself, frantically shuffling through his notes. "William had an important career in the Air Force. He said he was invited by Buckingham Palace to be the Queen's personal bodyguard."

Penny pressed on as the Peppers got hotter and more uncomfortable under the lights.

"After dismissal from the RAF for –" she checked her notes – "'dangerous and reckless wing-walking over Buckingham Palace as a dare', he married an eccentric Austrian duchess. They didn't get on and William finally turned up at Starcross, penniless."

"No!" shouted Martin, standing up now and shaking his little hamster fist. "William wouldn't do that!"

Penny continued reading from her sheet. "The duchess gave birth to a baby boy named Hector in an Austrian castle. Not being the mothering type, she placed him in a picnic basket and popped him in the post back to Starcross Hall, putting an end to the problem. This is how you, Lord Pepper, came to appear on the doorstep with nothing but a birth certificate and a clean nappy."

Lord Pepper's face drained of colour. "Oh. The servants never mentioned that."

"But, dear viewers, this is where it gets really interesting," said Penny, turning to the camera, a curious smile playing around the edge of her lips. "According to our evidence, on William's last day at Starcross, he and his father had the most terrible argument. William stormed out, leaving his baby behind and taking the family jewels instead. The next thing we know, he is exchanging those very jewels for *The Silver Phantom* at auction – *the plane which will carry him to his DOOM!"*

The library doors flew open with a terrific clatter and the temperature in the library plunged to freezing. William Pepper whipped in like a whirlwind, tearing round the library, knocking books flying off the shelves and rattling the chandeliers. The piano lid flew up and down and the keys crashed in dischord. *"HOW DARE YOU!"*

Penny looked most annoyed at the interruption. "Hattie," she complained. "What a gale! These places are like draughty old barns. DOORS, please. We're filming! Someone fetch my coat and turn the heaters on."

"Madam!" William shouted in Penny's face, blowing her hair back. "What ROT! These accusations are outrageous! You, madam, are a liar and a disgrace. Where is your proof? I am William Pepper, Lord of Starcross, and I ask you to kindly leave my home right this moment!"

Penny smoothed her hair down and sniffed at the air. "Can anyone else smell aniseed?" she asked, wrinkling her nose, her eyes roaming around the room. "I can definitely smell aniseed and – *poo* – it's awful. Does anyone have any air freshener?"

The ghost of William stood over Penny, infuriated, stamping his foot in a tantrum. "Can you not hear me, woman?" he bellowed into the fluffy microphone on a stick. "Are you cloth-eared, madam? I said leave right now! I forbid you from coming to my family home and spouting poppycock. Martin, come down here and show this intruder the edge of your blade!"

But Martin didn't move, just frowned. "What does she mean about the family jewels, William?" he called down from the shelf. "Is she right? Did you *really* steal them? Because you always used to say that stealing was very wrong."

"ME? Steal? No-no-no-no-noooo, of course not." William controlled his temper for a moment and forced a charming grin to spread across his face like sunshine. "Well, not really. I saw it more as *borrowing*. They were technically mine, after all, weren't they? Don't listen to her, old chum, load of old drivel. All a misunderstanding. Fuss and nonsense. Storm in a teacup."

Martin pressed on. "But what about baby Hector? You did mean to come back and take care of him, didn't you?"

William threw his arms up in the air in exasperation and the smile slipped behind a black cloud of irritation. "For goodness' sake! I couldn't be expected to stay and look after a crying baby, could I? I'm an adventurer,

a hero – I have a medal!"

Martin put his notebook away and fell silent. The little hamster jumped off the shelf, crossed the room and stood very close to Knitbone.

Meanwhile, ever professional and not put off by the windy conditions, Penny pressed on with the interview. "Lord Pepper, I am here to tell you that your father was *not* a hero, but a disgrace to the Pepper family name." She turned dramatically towards the camera and stared into it. "*Which brings us to the most shocking revelation of all.*" With a dramatic flourish, she handed over a yellowing letter. "This personal letter is dated the night that William turned his back on Starcross once and for all, sealing his fate. It is from his father, Lord Albert Pepper. Please read it aloud to the camera."

Lord Pepper took out his glasses and began.

16th August 1965

Dearest Cousin Adelia,

As you know, I had high hopes for my only son,
William. However, I am sorely disappointed to report
that he seems to have transformed into a reckless,
irresponsible fool. There has been a dishonourable
military discharge, a disastrous marriage to a daft
duchess and now a baby son has turned up in a picnic
basket. Honestly, have you ever heard of such a thing?
Delivered like a pint of milk to my doorstep! There
was a dreadful scene and now William has stormed
off with the family jewels. It's too much.

Therefore, it is with great regret that I have decided
to disinherit my son. I hereby leave Starcross Hall,

land and contents to you on my death, as my
favourite cousin. I am a very old man – my days
are numbered and I'm much too tired for all
this nonsense.

Yours affectionately,
Lord Albert Pepper

PS Thanks for the mittens.

Lord Pepper looked at Penny, most distraught
and confused. "What does this mean?"

"This means, Hector Pepper, as William flew
to his doom in The Silver Phantom, not only was
he not a hero, he wasn't even the heir to
Starcross Hall. Which means…" Penny stood up
and held her arms aloft. "*This is not your house!*"

Winnie strode defiantly into shot. "Don't be ridiculous. Of course it is. It's our home. Who else's could it be?"

Hattie the researcher, who had been watching from the shadows, stepped into the spotlight.

She folded her arms and announced:

"Starcross Hall is *mine*."

# Chapter 16

## WOLF

Harriet glared triumphantly at the Peppers. "My real name is Harriet Pepper, and I am the rightful owner of Starcross Hall."

"But...but...you can't be! I've never even heard of you!" said Lord Pepper, reeling from the information, his voice getting rather shrill.

"You are an imposter!" cried Lady Pepper in outrage. "A wolf in sheep's clothing! And to think I gave you some of my special home-made mossy marmalade!"

Harriet stood up very straight and glared at her. "My name is Harriet Spatula Pepper. I am your third cousin and rightful heir to the Starcross Estate." She took the letter and waved it under Lord Pepper's nose. "My grandmother, Adelia, being as bonkers as you, clearly never took that letter seriously, slipping it into her knitting bag, carrying it with her mitten mountain, never giving it a second thought. After she died I was searching through her things, looking for anything that I could sell – paintings, jewellery, furs – when I struck gold. So many years wasted in a rickety shack, living off cabbage soup, while you lived in the family home, calling yourself Lord and Lady. Like a panther I waited and watched, biding my time, waiting for the perfect time to pounce." She was pacing around the library now for dramatic effect. It was clear she worked in television.

"My job is to research. Good research takes

patience, and mine was most thorough. When I heard about *The Silver Phantom* through the antiques grapevine – that they had discovered William's final resting place – it was all too perfect. Penny and Toby the director agreed to help as they knew it would make the best episode of *Junk Palace* ever, the news being beamed into millions of living rooms across the world." She picked up a tiara from the top of the piano and popped it on her head. "At last I have my very own Junk Palace, and everyone will know it's rightfully mine. *Lady Hattie* sounds much better than

Lady Winnie, don't you think?"

"CUT!" shouted Toby the director. "It's a wrap! Such drama! Fabulous stuff, darlings. The best *Junk Palace* ending ever!"

"Is this a joke?" asked Lord Pepper as the spotlights were turned off one by one, leaving him in the dark. "Is it some sort of stunt for the television?"

"Look, we just need to sort this mistake out," said Winnie, marching across the room to her parents. "Dad, just show her the paperwork that proves that Starcross is ours and put an end to this nonsense once and for all."

There was a long silence in which Lord Pepper looked very worried. "The thing is," he said, "I'm much better at hats than paperwork. All I know is that I was sent away to boarding school aged four."

"Really?" implored Winnie. "You have nothing? No paperwork at all?"

"The label in my school blazer said *Lord Hector Pepper of Starcross Hall*, if that helps."

Winnie put her head in her arms. Hattie had stitched them up like kippers. When she looked up again, men were carrying sofas and boxes through the big doors. "What's going on *now*?" she cried.

"The vans weren't full of filming equipment at all, Winnie!" Knitbone barked. "This was her plan all along – Hattie's moving in today! Why-oh-why didn't I say something? She seemed so friendly but I KNEW there was something wrong about her, right from the start. A dog's instinct never lies." Knitbone let out a long and miserable howl.

To add to the chaos, the walkie-talkie on Winnie's belt sprang into life as a deep voice crackled over the airwaves: "Pilot Alan here. Filming's over and it's time to return the aircraft to the RAF museum. *Silver Phantom* returning to base. Do you read me? I repeat: *Silver Phantom* returning to base. OVER AND OUT."

William, who had been in a deep sulk up to this point, brightened up instantly. "What was that? *The Silver Phantom*'s returning to base?" He jumped up in the air and cheered. "WOO-HOO! At last – free spirits are *go*! Being a stuffy old lord was never my idea of fun anyway." William swept past them towards the doorway, whistling a chirpy tune, waving his leather-gloved hand in farewell. "Goodbye! Goodbye!"

Winnie stood in line with the Beloveds, watching William's retreat with a great sense of relief. "Phew," she whispered through gritted teeth. "Well at least *something* good has happened."

"Yes," Valentine grinned and waved. "I was beginning to think we'd never get rid of him."

"Eez for the good, so do not be sobby, my little sad-face friend." Orlando put his arm around

Martin's shoulders and gave him a squeeze.

Then, at the last moment, William turned around. "Are you ready then, Martin?"

Martin looked startled. "What do you mean?"

William rolled his eyes. "It's time for us to GO."

Martin stared. "Go? You want me to come with you?"

"Well, of course!" William cried, as if it was the most obvious thing in the world. "You're my Beloved, aren't you? Say goodbye to Starcross."

# Chapter 17

# WE'LL MEET AGAIN

There was a long, shocked silence, eventually broken by Valentine.

"William, you can't ask him to do this! It's too dangerous to cross the Starcross Estate boundaries," he spluttered. "Remember the rules: it would result in Oblivion. There would be nothing left of him!"

"Martin's staying right where he is. It's not safe to leave," said Gabriel, folding his wings across his chest and holding his head high.

"*We* are your family, aren't we, Martin?"

"Yes. It's the most pointless and selfish idea I've ever heard." Valentine gave a hollow laugh. "Martin, tell him it's impossible."

But Martin said nothing, just shuffled his feet miserably and fiddled with his sword.

"Martin?" whimpered Knitbone, a bad feeling creeping into his tail. "Just tell William you're *not* leaving, please."

Martin gazed up at William for a long moment. "We ARE still best friends, aren't we, William, like in the photograph? That's why you kept it, isn't it? Do you remember our games? How we swore to protect Starcross Hall?" But William wasn't paying attention, distracted by the deep rumble of the twin engines being fired up. Martin didn't give up though, speaking in a louder voice. "William, do you remember how lonely you were when I died? How you cried and said you'd love me for ever?"

Like a wave, Knitbone felt the fear wash through his tail and down to his toes as he realized what was about to happen. "Please, Martin, listen," he begged, the whites of his eyes shining. "Think about this. You can't leave us."

Orlando wrapped his arms around Martin, burying his face in his fur. "No, no my hammy friend, you cannot go. Orlando LOFFS you!"

"Martin, listen to me very carefully!" Gabriel gabbled, flapping his wings. "William is a poltergeist. Do you hear me? A POLTERGEIST! He isn't the kind boy you used to play with any more, he's someone else now – he's a bad spirit. I'm sorry, but I don't think he loves you now. That was the old William. You can't go with this terrible man!"

Martin shrugged his little furry shoulders and gave a deep and weary sigh. "But don't you see that I must?" he said. "Isn't that what true friendship is all about – sticking with each other through thick and thin? William might be a bit different these days, but he is still my special person. I can't turn my back on him, it's my duty."

Martin turned to look at his friends, his little black eyes wet and shiny. "Please try to be brave. Don't worry about me or be scared. It probably won't hurt at all. Or maybe just a little bit."

"No, Martin," pleaded Winnie, her bottom lip wobbling. "Please, don't go. WE need you more than William does. Who's going to help us fight Hattie? Don't break up the gang, it'll never be the same without you." She looked at the others in desperation. "Look, I know, we could try harder to be friends with William. He can stay if it's that important. I'll sleep in the attic. I don't mind."

Martin smiled and shook his head. "Wonderful Winnie Pepper, I'm sorry about the bedroom, the party and…stuff." He turned to the others. "Valentine, you're in charge of the biscuit cupboard from now on. Don't forget: ginger nuts

on top, ginger creams below. Gabriel, you can have my soldier comics for the library, I know you'll take good care of them. Orlando, I want you to take care of my spyglass, because you'll keep it smart and shiny." He handed it to Orlando, who plopped fat tears all over it.

Then Martin turned to Knitbone and patted his leg. "You're a good boy and I'm very sorry we fell out. You're going to have to guard Starcross from now on, so you might need this." He drew his little wooden sword from his belt and handed it to Knitbone.

Martin gulped down the lump in his throat, his voice small and trembly. "Goodbye, my dear

and special friends." And with this, Martin leaped up into William's outstretched palm and they began sprinting towards the open door of the moving plane.

"NOOOOO!" wailed Orlando, racked with sobs.

Winnie picked the little monkey up and held him in her arms. "You have to let him go. It's what he wants."

"But eez NOT what *I* want!" shouted Orlando. "Eez NOT what *you* want!" He pounded his little fists against Winnie, his eyes popping. "This is biggest and baddest podlob EVER. I know him all his life *and* death – we must stop him or he will go DRIPPY!" Orlando wriggled and twisted and slipped out of Winnie's grasp like a wet fish. "Martin!" he cried. "Orlando will save you!"

"NO! Come back!" howled Knitbone as they all broke into a run, hearts pounding as they dodged around the removal men.

They ran as fast as they could, panting and
gasping, but they were too late. By the time they
reached the front lawn *The Silver Phantom* was
gathering speed as it taxied across the field, its
propellers whirring. Orlando ran and hopped
alongside, desperately trying to get Martin's

attention. "MARTIN! TELL POLTYGOOSED I
SWAP MY VERY BESTEST SPOON FOR YOU!!"

Martin appeared at the window, waving
William's handkerchief and looking as if his heart
was breaking.

*The Silver Phantom* raced along the lawn, faster and faster, until eventually it tilted into the air and took off, engines roaring. It glinted in the sunlight and climbed up-up-up into a cloudless sky, soaring and looping the loop.

"Pilot Alan is writing something in the sky," cried Winnie, shielding her eyes from the sun. "Look!" A ribbon of vapour letters streamed out behind it…

The silence seemed to go on for ever. The Silver Phantom got smaller and smaller, tugging their heartstrings across the sky.

"Can it be true?" murmured Gabriel. "That our little soldier has really, really gone?"

Valentine lowered his head, his ears and

whiskers drooping. "Nothing at Starcross will ever be the same again."

Knitbone howled and howled and howled at the sky. They all stood in a huddle, their arms, wings and paws around each other, drenched in the most terrible sadness.

## Chapter 18

# PLANE SAILING

"I can't believe it," said Valentine.

"Neither can I," whimpered Knitbone.

"None of us can," said Winnie, wiping her eyes. "It doesn't seem real that we'll never see him again."

"No, I *mean*," said Valentine, suddenly standing on tiptoe, squinting, his long ears standing to attention. "I CAN'T BELIEVE IT!" Valentine had extremely good eyesight. He pointed towards the horizon. "Look!"

"What?" they chorused.

"OVER THERE!" cried
Valentine, breaking into
a powerful sprint. "Over
there in the sky!"

Everyone squinted into
the distance. There, just
over the Starcross bus
stop, was a tiny dot floating
down to earth.

"NO!" laughed Winnie, clamping her hand
over her mouth, hardly daring to hope. "It can't
be!"

"Is that who I think it is?" barked Knitbone
in delight, his tail wagging so fast it was no more
than a blur.

"*MY FATTY-RATTY FRIEND!*" squealed
Orlando and they galloped across the fields.

The little figure drifted through the sky like
a plump piece of thistledown. He landed just

inside the Estate boundary, with an *oof* and an *ouch*, gathering up the handkerchief parachute behind him.

"Oh, Martin! What a relief!" They all rushed around him, pushing and shoving to be the first to give him a hug. Valentine picked him up, gave him a big squeeze and said, "Don't you *ever, ever* do that to us again. You really scared us!"

Winnie's face was all smiles. "I'm so glad you're alright! What made you change your mind, Martin?"

Martin slipped into the grass and dusted off his knees. "William, actually."

"But I thought it was your duty to go with him?"

"Well," said Martin sheepishly, "high altitude is amazingly good for clearing the mind. I realized some important stuff up there in the clouds." He looked up at the horizon to see that *The Silver Phantom* had disappeared into the sky and out of their lives for ever. Martin watched for a moment and gave a little salute to the heavens. Then he turned to his friends. "William let an important piece of information slip up there, and suddenly I remembered rule number one on the Handy Hints and Tips For New Beloveds sheet: *Beloveds will defend their home to the last.*"

He looked up at Knitbone. "I'll be needing that sword back, thank you." Knitbone handed it over gladly. Martin slipped it into its scabbard, hitched up his belt and said, "Follow me, comrades. Quick march."

As they reached the house, the last of Hattie's possessions were being unloaded from the van and carried inside. Bewildered by the morning's events, Lord and Lady Pepper stood on the doorstep, suitcases in hand, looking like grown-up evacuees.

"Oh, for goodness' sake, Peppers, don't be so wet," said Hattie. "I'm sure you'll get used to living in a hovel somewhere. I've already called you a taxi and it will be here any moment." She picked up the Pepperwhacker cane. "This was in the library." She flung it at Lord Pepper, who just managed to catch it. "You can keep it as a souvenir of the day you lost Starcross."

Martin looked up at Knitbone. "Right. Listen carefully – these are your orders. Stay here and fix an eye on the sky. Whatever you do, *don't let Hattie get it.*"

"The sky? What do you mean, Martin? I don't know what's going on," said Knitbone, looking at the others. "Get what?"

"A paper plane. There's no time to explain because the taxi will be here any minute. You'll just have to trust me." Martin turned to the others. "Valentine, I'll need your paws for the folds. Gabriel, come with me, I need you to be on lookout. Winnie, it's your job to keep Hattie busy for the next few minutes." Martin looked up at Knitbone with a steely glare, pointing his sword. "*You must catch it.* Hattie mustn't get to it first – understood? Good luck, team." With that, Martin shot up the stairs, Gabriel and Valentine following closely behind.

Hattie spotted Winnie standing in the courtyard. "Oh look, it's the little Lady." She grinned.

"You pretended to be my friend," said Winnie, tilting up her proud chin, "but all the time you were plotting against us. You have no honour."

Hattie chuckled. "Oh dear, I must say I'm disappointed in you, Winifred. I thought you had more spirit than that." She lowered her face until it was very close to Winnie's. For the first time Winnie noticed that Hattie smelled of stale coffee and old doughnuts. "If there's one thing that life has taught me it's that you don't need

*honour* when you are in possession of the facts."
Hattie held up the ageing letter from the
interview and waved it about with glee. Her
laugh was bright and brittle. "Here it is, in
black-and-white, dated, stamped and sent by that
old miser, Lord Albert Pepper. Have you found
a scrap of evidence to prove that Starcross Hall
is yours yet?" she spat, looking Winnie up and
down in disgust. "You shabby little urchin? No?
Of course you haven't, because there isn't any.
When it comes to property and titles, there's
nothing like hard evidence, you know."

"Winnie, NOW!" barked Knitbone, his head
tilted to the skies.

Winnie looked up to see Martin and Valentine
standing on a ledge, launching a paper plane out
of her open bedroom window.

The plane plummeted down towards the
courtyard like a white bird. It looped the loop
and circled a few times above their heads.

"What's going on?" demanded Harriet, squinting into the spring sunshine. "What's that thing?" Hattie reached up to snatch it but Winnie, thinking quickly, stamped hard on her foot.

Knitbone heard Martin's command loud in his head: *You MUST catch it*. He loved catching things and he was good at it too. He and Winnie had practised for hours when he was alive. With Hattie hopping around in pain, Knitbone leaped up and caught it effortlessly like a frisbee, passing it straight into Winnie's waiting palm.

Winnie unfolded it and smoothed it out flat on the front step. It was a document, handwritten in black ink on creamy headed paper, embossed with the Pepper coat of arms. At the top it said: *Last Will and Testament of Lord Albert Pepper.*

Harriet's eyes were bulging. "Let me see that," she spat, grasping at the paper in vain.

But Winnie held it out of reach and began to read the contents out loud in front of everyone – the Peppers, the crew and the ghosts.

Last Will and Testament of Lord Albert Pepper
16th August 1968

Dearest William,
You have been missing for three years today and I'm afraid I fear the worst. But, should you ever return, I want to tell you that I greatly regret our falling out and my hasty decisions. Now, as I lie here on my

deathbed, your dear mother also departed from this earth, I want to put things right before it's too late.

Some people are suited to a life of duty and some are not. I have now decided to leave Starcross Hall, the land and contents to your baby son, Hector. He is turning out to be a fine little boy and I think you would be proud of him. I am putting this in the hands of Finias, my trusted old butler, who has promised to keep it safe until he sees you again. This is my last word on the matter.

Until we meet again, in this world or the next,

With love,
Lord Albert Pepper (Papa)

"NO. It can't be real," gasped Hattie, sweating like an old cheese. "I've been through all the records! For the last three days I've searched this house from top to bottom. I've checked and double-checked and triple-checked. Research is my job – I don't make mistakes and there was not a scrap of evidence anywhere!"

"Sorry, Hattie," said Winnie, holding the letter out of reach. "Here it is in black-and-white, written and signed *exactly three whole years* after your letter. It's definitely the most up-to-date proof of who owns Starcross, I'm afraid." Winnie beamed and gave a big wink. "When it comes to property and titles, there is nothing like hard evidence, you know."

With a wildcat screech, Hattie made a furious grab at Winnie. But, to everyone's amazement, Lord Pepper stepped forward and planted himself firmly between them. He held the Pepperwhacker up above his head and snapped it in half with a loud *crack!* Everyone stood open-mouthed – Hector Pepper had never done anything so heroic in his whole life! "Don't you DARE touch her. Winifred Clementine Violet Araminta Pepper is the true and only heir to Starcross Hall. I'm afraid your little plan has failed," he boomed. "GET OFF OUR LAND!"

And everyone cheered.

Chapter 19

# PiCTURE PERFECT

The newly-painted portrait of William in the library was very dashing. He was in uniform, his moustache waxed into two curls and his blue eyes twinkling with trouble. Winnie and the Beloveds all stood in the library, looking up at it and getting a crick in the neck.

"He looks every inch the hero, doesn't he, that grandfather of mine?"

"As the saying goes, you should never judge a book by its cover," said Knitbone. "*Junk Palace* wasn't what it seemed, either. I think I might watch nature programmes on Sunday instead from now on. You know where you are with a twitchy squirrel."

Martin sighed. "I hope William's alright. I'm sure he'll feel at home back at the aircraft museum. He told me there were other human ghosts there too, pilots that waved from their windows." He looked up at Knitbone and gave a long sigh. "I tried so hard to make him happy. I lost my head there for a while, didn't I?" The smell of peppermint wafted through the air.

"Don't be daft, Martin," woofed Knitbone. "Beloveds are the most loyal of all ghosts. You couldn't help it. You were only doing your job."

"That was a close call, though," said Martin. "What if William hadn't boasted about Hattie's mistake at the last minute, up there in the clouds? I couldn't believe my ears when he

admitted that Finias had told him about the
inheritance letter at the party. How could he not
say anything to us, even as Hattie was claiming
that Starcross was hers?" Martin frowned.

"The worst of it all is he didn't even care. He only cared about causing trouble. That was the moment I knew I had to jump out of the plane. I couldn't let you down in your hour of need, could I? 'A Beloved defends his home to the last'. That's a very important rule."

"Well, we're very glad too," said Gabriel. "Imagine, all that time we were arguing with William at the midnight feast, Finias really *did* have something important to say. Proof of Starcross ownership was right under our feet for all those years!"

"All that scrabbling at the floorboards and mumbling makes sense now," said Winnie. "The butler certainly found a good hiding place for the will. A bit TOO good!"

"I bet Finias was delighted when William's ghost turned up," said Valentine. "He must have been the first in the queue for that party. Finally he could let go of his secret."

Martin climbed up onto the top of the piano and picked up the old black-and-white photograph from the plane. With his little pink paw he traced the picture of himself with William, sitting on the steps of Starcross all those years ago.

"I will always miss my boy," he said in a quiet voice, "but he is never coming back." Then he looked over at his friends and smiled. "I might be a ghost, but I don't belong in the past. I belong here now, with you, my family. I've learned that looking backwards sometimes means you just fall over."

At this moment they were interrupted by
a loud, gurgly rumble erupting from Martin's
tummy.

"Hooray!" squealed Orlando, as he
cartwheeled across the piano lid. "Now I know
my friend is *really* back!"

"I am!" Martin laughed and loosened his belt.
"Now, who's for a biscuit banquet? I'm dead
hungry!"

# MEET THE AUTHOR

Claire Barker is an author, even though she has terrible handwriting. When she's not busy doing this, she spends her days wrestling sheep, battling through nettle patches and catching rogue chickens. She used to live on narrowboats but now lives with her delightful family and an assortment of animals on a small, unruly farm in deepest, darkest Devon.

# MEET THE ILLUSTRATOR

Ross Collins is the illustrator of over a hundred books, and the author of a dozen more. Some of his books have won shiny prizes which he keeps in a box in Swaziland. The National Theatre's adaptation of his book "The Elephantom" was rather good, with puppets and music and stuff. Ross lives in Glasgow with a strange woman and a stupid dog.

# Everyone's barking mad for Knitbone Pepper, Ghost Dog

"Full of hilarity, warmth and undefeated love...
a singularly beautiful book!"
Middle Grade Strikes Back

"My time at Starcross has been
truly spectacular – in fact,
I would go so far as to say
it was MAGIC!"

The Amazing Umbonzo,
Master Illusionist & Magician

"Darling Isadora, did you see on the
interweb-thing? Knitbone Pepper,
Ghost Dog was selected by
Mumsnet as one of their
best books!"
Lord Pepper

"Winnie Pepper is a real bobby dazzler! What a star!"
Penny Farthing, top presenter of Junk Palace

"With its sweet ghost animals and ginger-nut-fuelled adventure, this charming story ticks all the right boxes."
Love Reading 4 Kids

"Someone needs to stop feeding those ghosts pink wafers. Pesky troublemakers!"
Krispin O'Mystery, Ghost Hunter Extraordinaire

"I would highly recommend that you invite the Pepper family into your life and enjoy the rollercoaster of the ride that this adventure provides."
Book Lover Jo

Collect ALL the adventures of

KNITBONE
PEPPER
GHOST DOG

## Meet Knitbone Pepper, the lovable ghost dog!

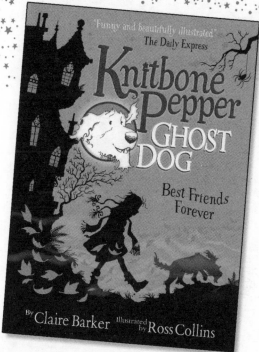

"Funny and beautifully illustrated"
The Daily Express

Knitbone
Pepper
GHOST
DOG

Best Friends
Forever

By Claire Barker Illustrated by Ross Collins

Knitbone has made lots of new animal friends since becoming a ghost dog. But his owner, Winnie, is missing him.

Can the ghostly gang come up with a plan in time to help Winnie see Knitbone again?

ISBN 9781474931984    www.usborne.com/fiction

# Roll up! Roll up!
## The circus is coming to Starcross!

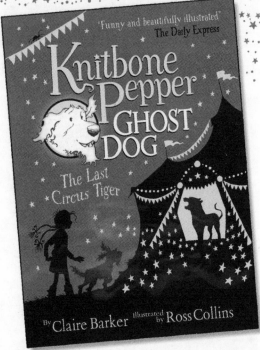

'Funny and beautifully illustrated'
The Daily Express

# Knitbone Pepper
# GHOST DOG

The Last Circus Tiger

By Claire Barker  Illustrated by Ross Collins

Winnie and her ghostly animal friends
can't wait. The magicians, acrobats
and clowns are such fun!

But Knitbone sniffs something
beastly in the big top...

ISBN 9781474931991          www.usborne.com/fiction

# Meet Moon,
## Knitbone's new friend!

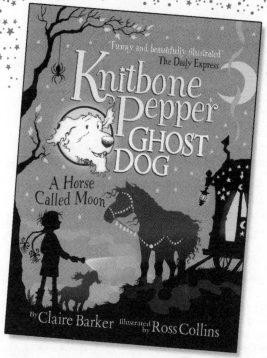

One starry night, Winnie and Knitbone Pepper
find a ghost horse hiding in the garden. Her name is
Moon, and she is searching for her long-lost owner.

But Moon has a spooky secret,
which is sure to spell trouble.

ISBN 9781474932004    www.usborne.com/fiction

First published in the UK in 2019 by Usborne Publishing Ltd.,
Usborne House, 83-85 Saffron Hill, London EC1N 8RT, England. www.usborne.com

A CIP catalogue record for this book is available from the British Library.

ISBN 9781474953528  J MAMJJASOND/19  05123/1
Printed in the UK.